2nd Year Class Library.

THE NEW WINDMILL SERIES

General Editors: Anne and Ian Serraillier

294

CHARLIE MOON AND
THE BIG BONANZA BUST-UP

CHARLIE
MOON
AND
THE BIG
BONANZA
BUST-UP

written and illustrated by

Shirley Hughes

HEINEMANN EDUCATIONAL BOOKS
LONDON

Heinemann Educational Books Ltd
22 Bedford Square, London WC1B 3HH

LONDON   EDINBURGH   MELBOURNE   AUCKLAND
HONG KONG   SINGAPORE   KUALA LUMPUR   NEW DELHI
IBADAN   NAIROBI   JOHANNESBURG   KINGSTON
PORTSMOUTH (NH)   PORT OF SPAIN

ISBN 0 435 12294 0

Printed and bound in Great Britain by
William Clowes Limited, Beccles and London

Characters in this Story

Charlie Moon, a boy hero

Ariadne, his cousin

Dodger Best, his friend

Linda, a lovely children's librarian

Norman, Charlie's uncle,
temporarily employed as a waiter

Owen Bowen, Linda's uncle, an artist

Mr Dix, Owen Bowen's landlord, an art dealer

Duggie Bubbles, a famous TV magician

Charlie's Mum, a hairdresser

Trevor and Ray, two mysterious men

A Lady Illustrator

For all children's librarians
with admiration and gratitude

Contents

1 Bonanza Blues

It was pitch dark inside. Charlie couldn't see anything except a bit of back belonging to his friend, Dodger Best. They were trying hard to walk out of step. It wasn't easy. Charlie hung on to the belt of Dodger's jeans and stumbled along as best he could but he kept falling over Dodger's feet. Dodger's muffled voice came back to him through the stuffy blackness telling him what to do.

"Come on, Charl. It's like the opposite of marching, see. I lead with the left foot and you go off on the right. Ready?"

"O.K., but go a bit quicker, will you?"

They started off again, one two, one two. Charlie kept remembering a poem he knew:

"Will you walk a little faster?" said a whiting to a snail. "There's a porpoise close behind us, and he's treading on my tail."

There wasn't a porpoise behind them, but an even stranger creature: Charlie's cousin Ariadne, wearing her home-made robot suit. He could hear her breathing heavily as she clanked along.

"Faster, Dodger," he urged.

"I can't."

"Go *on*."

Dodger suddenly quickened his pace alarmingly. Now he was going too fast for Charlie to keep up. They lurched forward, quite out of control. Then, without

(11)

warning, Dodger stopped dead. Charlie's left foot tangled with his right one. They swayed about, trying to keep their balance. Ariadne, stepping up briskly behind, cannoned straight into them. There was a great tinny crash, a ripping of cloth, a thudding of wild kicks. Under a rain of heavy objects they all hit the floor.

Charlie was the one underneath. He couldn't even struggle. He just lay there trying not to be squashed to death by Dodger and promising himself never to be the back legs of anything ever again. Especially not a horse. More especially not if Dodger was the front legs. He wasn't a reliable person to go about with at the best of times, what with holding his breath between one lamp-post and another on the way to school or suddenly deciding to sidle about like a crab. You never knew when he was going to have a stop-and-go phase. Being inside the same skin with him was a mistake from the beginning, thought Charlie bitterly. Next time, at the very least, it was front legs or nothing.

At last Linda, the children's librarian, wrestling with zips and fastenings, managed to rescue them and get them on to their feet. There were books all over the place. They'd been accidentally knocked off a nearby display stand. Luckily all this had happened in the small room across the passage from the main library, the one where Linda sometimes read stories aloud to them. The door was firmly shut, so the people who were choosing their books didn't rush across to demand who was making all the noise. Even so, Linda looked anxiously towards the door.

"Come on, you three, we'd better get this lot tidied up right away," she said. "Charlie, Dodger, you start piling up all those books—very carefully, mind—and I'll re-arrange them as they were. Ariadne, you'd better get the costumes back into their boxes. I hope nothing's been damaged. The horse suit is only borrowed and I've promised to return it in good condition."

Linda had borrowed the costumes for the Book Bonanza which was going to be at the end of this half-term week. She had hired the big hall which was next door to the library, and there were going to be lots of stands with all kinds of books on them—ghost books and fairy-tale books and books about snakes and racing cars and magic and Egyptian mummies and monsters from outer space. There were going to be badges and stickers and some real writers and artists too. Linda was organizing it all. She had a lot of good ideas, like having some people in fancy dress walking up and down outside the hall with notices telling everyone about the Book Bonanza and getting them to come inside. This was where Charlie, Dodger and Ariadne came in. Today was supposed to be a sort of rehearsal.

"Thank goodness my notice is O.K.," said Ariadne, leaning it tenderly up against a wall. "It took me hours to do. Typical of you to go falling over it, Charlie Moon." She always thought that things which happened to Charlie quite accidentally were "typical". It was her favourite word. The other was "pathetic". Worse still, she'd just discovered another one: "nauseating". "You're absolutely *nauseating*," she would tell Charlie, whenever she could steer the conversation round to it. He wasn't quite sure yet what it meant, but he knew it wasn't a compliment.

They got the books back on to the shelves. Linda looked worried. Her hair was all on end. It was short and curly all over like a red setter that's been out in the rain, only it smelt much nicer.

"There's only a few days to go and so much to do," she said.

"Is Duggie Bubbles really coming?" asked Charlie and Dodger for about the twentieth time.

Everyone knew about Duggie Bubbles because they'd all seen him doing magic tricks on television. He was going to be the star attraction of the Bonanza. Charlie was planning to be a television conjuror too, so he was anxious to pick up some hints. You were supposed to have a top hat, which Charlie hadn't, but he was working on that. He'd also spent his Christmas book-token on a book by Duggie Bubbles himself called *Magic for Boys and Girls*. But the chapter about cutting a hole in a large white handkerchief hadn't been a success because he'd kept getting the hole the wrong size. Mum had been very cross when she'd found out what had happened to all her good linen handkerchiefs.

"Yes, he's really coming," said Linda, "and so is that lady illustrator. They're going to use the platform. Everything's got to be absolutely ready by then. Oh, dear!"

They all liked Linda. She could read aloud ever so well. Listening to her was as good as a play. Dodger sometimes hung about at the back pretending he was doing something else, but really his ears were flapping. They all wanted to help with the Bonanza. But now it was nearly time for the library to close, so it was too late to do any more today.

They were just finishing tidying up when there was a great roaring noise outside. A powerful engine spluttered a couple of times and then shut off.

A fierce figure appeared in the doorway, covered from head to foot in shiny black plastic, with a helmet under its arm and its face covered like a bandit's with a white silk scarf. But inside it was only Norman, Charlie's young uncle. He quite often dropped in to collect Charlie from the library. This was because he hoped to linger about, chatting to Linda.

Charlie, Dodger and Ariadne ran out at once to admire Norman's big motorbike. Dodger stroked its shiny tank lovingly. Bending his knees and gripping imaginary handle-bars, he pretended to zoom off, leaning over sideways as he cornered at 80 m.p.h.

"I hope he's brought the spare crash helmet so I can have a ride," said Charlie.

This afternoon they were all in luck. Linda had invited everyone to have tea with *her* uncle, Mr Owen Bowen. Unlike Charlie's Uncle Norman, who was young, Linda's uncle was very old. He was often at home and liked to be visited.

Norman was in a good mood.

"O.K., Charlie, get this helmet on. I'll give you a lift round there," he said. With Charlie snug and secure on the pillion, he kicked the starter and revved the engine very loudly two or three times.

"See you there, folks," shouted Charlie above the din, with a careless wave.

The admiring group on the pavement watched as they roared away up the quiet road and disappeared round the bend. Even Ariadne was impressed.

2 A Ghost is Heard

Linda's Uncle Owen Bowen lived quite nearby on the top floor of a big old house. He was lucky with his view because his room overlooked the most beautiful river in the world: the steely, oily, muddy, tidal, glittering River Thames. The other houses along this River Walk were mostly very grand. Some elegantly furnished rooms could be glimpsed through the freshly painted windows. But the house where Uncle Owen Bowen lived stuck out like a rotting tooth in a row of gleaming white ones. Bits of the front seemed to be falling off into the basement area. The windows of the downstairs rooms, which were all empty, had bedraggled lace curtains drawn tightly across them.

Charlie and Norman arrived first, of course, and had to wait on the pavement until Linda, Ariadne and Dodger came strolling along the River Walk to join them. The row of doorbells next to Uncle Owen Bowen's front door bore the fading names of lodgers who had all gone away. It was no good ringing any of them because they were all disconnected, like Uncle Owen himself. He never seemed to hear anything that went on down in the street. They had to shout up to the

windows for a long time before his face appeared over the balcony. Then he dropped the front door key down to them.

The most difficult thing about getting through the hall was the smell. Or smells. Was it tom cats, dead rats, mouldy kippers or simply very old socks? Or all four? It was hard to tell. Every time they came there the smells seemed to be different. Today there was an ancient heater at the bottom of the stairs which smoked and stank gently, adding to the already over-laden air. As usual, all the children held their noses on the way upstairs.

"I'b nod breadigg add all," Charlie told Dodger, scarlet in the face as they reached the first landing.

"Neidder ab I," answered Dodger between clenched teeth.

"Dawseatigg!" muttered Ariadne.

Uncle Owen Bowen was hovering outside his room at the top of the house, waiting to welcome them. What a relief it was to be there. Inside, with the door shut, there was no smell at all except for a pleasant whiff of oil paint and turpentine. It was a lovely room. From the balcony outside you could see right up to the great iron bridge with its fairy-tale towers, and the moored barges, and the river slipping past. Near the window Uncle Owen Bowen had his easel and his paints and brushes, neatly arranged upright in big jars. Charlie had never seen so many interesting objects collected in one room. There was the stuffed pike in a glass case, the brass letter-scales, the fourteen old clocks (none of them going), the banjo, the tailor's dummy and the model ship. There were also stacks and stacks of pictures, framed and unframed, not only hung all over the walls but leaning up against them too. Uncle Owen had painted quite a few of these himself. Hanging over the massive sideboard was a birdcage, inside which lived, not a parrot or a budgie, but Uncle Owen's best false teeth and his gold-rimmed glasses. His sight was bad, so he kept them there for safety in case he lost them.

"I've got in some rock cakes for your tea," said Uncle Owen Bowen. "The home help bought them for me."

They ate standing up or wandering about the room because all the tables were too full already to put plates on them. This suited everyone very well, especially Dodger. There was nothing he hated more than a set meal. Uncle Owen Bowen had given them up years ago.

"I like this picture," said Ariadne, pausing in front of the easel. "Are you working on it now, Mr Bowen?"

"Yes, yes. River with pleasure boat. Greens and

blues. Light's a bit unreliable today, though."

"It's lovely. I like the way the clouds are flying up out of the top of the canvas."

"It's coming along, coming along. Must get the paints away before Mr Dix comes. Said he might drop in later, and he'll be ever so cross if he sees them."

"Why *should* he be cross?" asked Ariadne, indignant.

"Mess—paint on the carpet—smells. He complains about the smells. Oh dear, yes."

"But oil paints smell lovely," said Linda.

"Doesn't like them." Uncle Owen Bowen's pale eyes started nervously. His chin disappeared into his neck rather like a goose, which gave him a permanently startled look anyway. The very mention of Mr Dix made him nervous. Mr Dix was the owner of the house. He had bought it with Uncle Owen Bowen in it. There had been some other lodgers too, but they hadn't liked the way Mr Dix had kept popping in to check up on their habits. So one by one they had all packed up and moved out until only Uncle Owen was left. He had lived there all his life and didn't know where to go.

"Mr Dix says that Beauty's making the hall smell," said Uncle Owen. Beauty was his old cat. "But I have to let her go up and down so she can get out through her cat door."

"That old stove down there's smoking badly," said Norman. "Looks a bit dodgy to me."

"No, no. Mr Dix gave that to me himself. Good of him. Second-hand of course but he said it had cost him a lot. Beauty feels the cold terribly, you know."

Charlie knew Mr Dix. He didn't seem like a specially good person. He lived on a barge which was moored nearby, and he was always shouting at Charlie and Dodger whenever they played near that part of the river. Mr Dix had bought Uncle Owen Bowen's house so he could move in himself and do the old place up as a posh hotel. But he couldn't get people to pay a lot of money to stay there if Uncle Owen was messing about on the top floor, painting pictures. Mr Dix kept suggesting to Uncle Owen that he should go into a Home, but he wouldn't. He had an old friend who was in one he said, where the head nurse was a regular sergeant-major. Nobody there was allowed to use a small box of water-colours, let alone oil paints. Charlie wondered why so many things that seemed worth doing counted as making a mess, like practising conjuring, or Norman taking his motorbike to pieces in the front room.

Ariadne asked Uncle Owen if they could see some more of his paintings. She was keen on art. Uncle Owen let them turn some of the canvases that were stacked against the wall face forwards so they could look at them. They were nearly all of the river: on misty days and grey days, or in sparkling sunshine, with boats going up and down, and the water all jumping points of light. They admired them all, one by one.

"Did you do this one too, Mr Bowen?" asked Norman with interest. He was looking at a small chalk drawing hanging on the wall opposite the window. It was of a young lady with dark red hair.

"No, no. That's very old. It's of my grandmother, Lily Bowen. Linda's great grandmother. The Stunner, she was called. She was an artist's model. Drawn and painted by all the famous artists of her time. Stunner was their nick-name for a good-looking young lady in those days, and she was the most stunning stunner of them all."

Linda happened to be standing next to the drawing. Turned towards the light she looked just like the lady in the picture, except that her hair was short and curly and Lily Bowen's was long.

"Lovely," said Norman. Charlie hadn't known until now that Norman was keen on art. He'd never mentioned it.

"I don't think I ever had a great grandmother," said Dodger. "I've got a gran, but we've moved such a lot that I don't see her very often."

(24)

"Lily used to live by the river," Uncle Owen told them. "She was a mudlark's daughter."

"What's a mudlark?" they all wanted to know.

"Poor people who used to go down to the river at low tide and search for things in the mud that they might be able to sell. Rubbish and things that people had thrown away. Coins sometimes, if they were lucky. A famous artist saw Lily when she was helping her mother with the mudlarking and cleaned her up so he could paint her."

"Did she marry him?" asked Ariadne promptly.

"No, no. He married someone else. A richer lady. And Lily married George Bowen who kept a pub. But she wasn't happy. Not happy at all, I'm afraid."

"Poor lady," said Ariadne.

"After she died," said Uncle Owen quietly, "her ghost was supposed to haunt the river at low tide, down where she used to do her mudlarking. The place where the famous artist first found her."

They all fell silent, looking at the little drawing. Outside the spring dusk was starting to fall and the colours of the opposite bank of the river, so bright an hour ago, were ebbing away to grey like the tide. Overhead there was a faint scuffling noise, like footsteps walking in tissue paper. They began on one side of the ceiling and worked their way slowly over to the other, paused, then started again, then stopped.

"Who's that up in the attic, Uncle Owen?" asked Linda.

3 Smells and More Smells

There was nobody else in the house at all, as far as Uncle Owen knew. But he had heard that noise at dusk before.

"The place is full of smells and now it's got strange noises as well. I can't make it out," he said. They listened again. Now the noise had stopped the silence seemed ghostly too. Charlie had a nasty chilly feeling in the back of his neck.

"Perhaps it's Beauty catching mice," suggested Ariadne nervously.

But Charlie knew it couldn't be Beauty because he'd seen her sitting on the railings down below in River Walk. He couldn't help thinking about that sad, dead Lily and wondering if, rather than haunting the river mud, she'd taken to following Uncle Owen Bowen about instead. Just then there was a louder, creaking step on the landing and a knock on the door that made them all jump.

"Afternoon, all," said Mr Dix, stepping in without being asked. He was not a welcome sight. But it was a relief, at least, that he wasn't a ghost.

Mr Dix wore heavy dark glasses. When you looked into his eyes all you saw were two tiny reflections of yourself. He also wore a peaked cap which he never removed, indoors or out. It made him look rather like a sea-captain, an idea which he encouraged because he liked standing about on the deck of the safely-moored barge where he lived, pretending he was at sea and bossing an imaginary crew. Very little of his face was visible except for his jutting jaw.

"Good afternoon, Mr Dix," said Uncle Owen, hovering about in front of his easel and paints in the hope that they wouldn't be noticed. But it was too late. Mr Dix was already bearing down on them.

"Sorry to see you've got those paints all over the place again," he said to Uncle Owen, ignoring the others. "I could smell them half way up the stairs, you know. I'm a reasonable man, I hope. Don't like to interfere with tenants. Never did. But this is my property and we can't have oil paint smelling the place out and getting all over the carpet, can we?"

"Not on the carpet," murmured Uncle Bowen, shuffling his feet. "Most careful, I do assure you. A cup of tea, Mr Dix?"

"Haven't time, I'm afraid. Madly busy. Just dropped in to remind you about that drawing."

"Drawing?"

"You know. The little chalk drawing of the girl over there."

"Yes, yes. My grandmother. We were just looking at it when . . . I was telling these young people here . . . I mean . . . Mr Dix is an art dealer, you know," Uncle Owen explained to his guests.

Mr Dix nodded briefly.

"I've managed to get a few pounds for your river paintings from time to time, haven't I, Mr Bowen? I just wondered if you'd decided to sell that little drawing. It's a bad time, of course, but I might be able to find a buyer for it."

"Er, no, I don't think so, Mr Dix, thank you very much. I'm rather fond of it, you see."

"Oh, Uncle, you *can't* sell The Stunner!" cried Linda. "I couldn't bear you to part with it!"

"Pity. I might be able to get quite a good price, you never know," said Mr Dix. "And, considering your rent arrears, Mr Bowen . . ."

"I think it may be quite valuable," said Uncle Owen Bowen, "by such a famous artist . . ."

"Pity it's not signed," said Mr Dix, "that brings the value down a lot, of course. But I tell you what. Let me

have it valued for you. I know an expert—a customer of mine—who'll do that for me as a favour. No charge. And there's no need for you to sell if you don't like the price."

"Well . . ." Uncle Owen took the drawing down from the wall and held it in his hands, peering at it.

"I can have it back to you the day after tomorrow," said Mr Dix persuasively. And somehow, before they knew it, he had the drawing under his arm.

"Oh, Uncle!" said Linda.

It was too late again.

"I'll just make another pot of tea," said Uncle Owen apologetically, as he shuffled off into the little kitchen next door.

"You needn't worry, dear," Mr Dix told Linda. "This drawing's quite safe with me, you know, safe as houses. In fact, it's probably a lot safer than with your uncle here, bless him. A dear old soul, we all know, but he's slipping a bit. Memory isn't what it was. Wandering." He tapped the side of his temple. "I've noticed it quite a bit recently. He shouldn't be here on his own, you know."

"I don't think his memory's that bad," said Linda. "He's certainly quite able to make up his mind about selling that drawing. And he doesn't have to if he doesn't want to."

Mr Dix ignored this remark.

"Shouldn't be on his own," he repeated. "I don't like it. As his landlord I feel responsible. Never know what kind of damage he's likely to do now he's getting so forgetful. And he can't look after the place properly, you know. The house smells terrible. I shall be in trouble with the Health authorities if I don't do something about it."

"He's got the home help once a week."

"Well, it's not enough. I wish you'd get him to reconsider a Home. Otherwise I may have to take action. See if you can't persuade him to be sensible, dear—face up to his age." He pressed Linda's arm in a familiar way but she withdrew it quickly.

"Well, I mustn't stop. Can't wait for your uncle to make the tea, I'm afraid," said Mr Dix coldly. "And get him to watch those messy oil paints, won't you?" Without saying goodbye he was off, clattering down the stairs with The Stunner under his arm. They all looked at the small empty patch on the wallpaper where she had hung.

"Perhaps she'll start haunting Mr Dix for a change," said Ariadne.

Dodger was getting restless. All this talk of paintings and people in olden times had begun to bore him. He was inventing a complicated game of hopscotch, using the faded bunches of flowers on Uncle Owen's carpet.

"Come on, Charlie," he said. "My Mum wants me back by half past six. Let's go and play out for a bit."

All three children said goodbye and thank-you to Uncle Owen Bowen before, holding their noses like divers, they rushed downstairs and into the street. It was good to be outside again and take in great gasps of river air. It wasn't dark yet, though some windows along the River Walk were already lighted and encouraging sounds of supper on the way and snatches of radio music floated out into the dusk. Between the street and the river embankment itself there were some bits of garden with low walls and railings. Some had rowing boats drawn up in them, some had flowers and white-painted

seats. The garden opposite where Uncle Owen Bowen
lived was full of weeds and tangled bushes. It had an old
rotting shed which Charlie and Dodger used as their
Club Headquarters when Mr Dix wasn't looking.

Charlie and Dodger started a game called "Fire Down Below". You had to move about without touching the ground, pulling yourself along the railings, balancing on walls, leaping from one gatepost to another. If your foot touched the pavement you were on fire. If it touched three times you were all burnt up. Ariadne climbed on to the shed roof. She was the umpire.

"You're burning!" she shouted to Charlie as he stumbled for a second, just brushing the ground with his toe. "You've lost one life! You're on fire!"

Charlie clung to the railings. It was a very realistic game. He could even smell the smoke. So could Ariadne. From where she was sitting she could see right over the river on one side and all the houses on River Walk on the other. Surely it wasn't pretend smoke she could smell?

It was real, all right. And it was pouring out of Uncle Owen Bowen's front door.

4 Fire Down Below!

"Fire!" shouted Ariadne.

Charlie and Dodger thought this was part of the game.

"Not fair! I never touched the ground," called Dodger.

"A real fire, you pathetic idiot! I can see the smoke." Ariadne was already scrambling down from the shed. Then Charlie realized what was happening.

"Come on, Dodger, quick!" he said.

Together they all ran back to Uncle Owen Bowen's front door. Black oily smoke was billowing out into the street.

"It's from that old stove, I think," cried Ariadne. "Oh, Charlie, whatever shall we do?"

"Better not try to go in there ourselves," said Charlie. "Must tell the others. They can't have smelled it yet up all those stairs. If only one of these doorbells worked." He was pressing them all frantically, one by one, but it was no good. He stepped back into the street. "Hey, Norman!" he yelled at the top of his voice. "Lindaaaaah!" Putting his fingers into his mouth, he managed one of his piercing whistles.

Greatly to their relief, the faces of Norman and Linda

popped over the balcony at once. How
lucky that they happened to be out
there in the dusk.

"Come down, quick, Norman! The
stove's catching fire!"

Norman's jaw dropped. He popped
back instantly. Very soon they heard
him in the hall.

"Stand back, you kids!" he shouted.

They scattered away up the street as Norman
burst out through the front door in a cloud of
fumes, carrying the old stove at arms' length.
He had thrown a blanket right over it to
smother the smoke and stop it from catching
fire in the draught and he had wrapped his
scarf round and round his hand and arm.
He was choking and coughing and his
eyes were streaming. He dumped
the stove on the pavement and
stood well back. After a moment
or two he managed to get close
enough to turn it off.

Gradually the smoke subsided. Norman collapsed against the railings, mopping his face with his scarf. The situation was saved. The whole operation had only taken a few minutes.

"Is the fire out?" asked Ariadne, scared.

"Yes. It didn't burst into flames, but it was just going to. Lucky you kids called me in time, or the whole house would have been on fire."

"You all right, Norman?" Linda's white face appeared in the doorway.

"I'm O.K. You'd better let your uncle know there's nothing to worry about. But tell him not to have any more old heaters in the house."

"Thank heaven the children saw the smoke. Oh, Norman, you've probably saved our lives!"

Norman only grinned at her.

Norman and Charlie were late for their supper that evening. They'd seen Linda and Ariadne off on the same bus.

Then Norman had gone ahead on his motorbike while Charlie walked home, saying goodnight to Dodger outside the big block of flats where he lived.

Charlie's home was over the shop where his Mum had her hairdressing business. Norman was living with them for the time being because he'd just left college and had come to London to look for a job. He'd been studying something called Philosophy but, although he and Charlie scanned the newspapers every evening, there never seemed to be any jobs advertised for Philosophers. So Norman was being a waiter, part-time, instead.

Charlie's Mum was a bit cross about them being late but she'd kept their supper hot: mince, tomatoes and mashed potatoes. Norman and Charlie were tired out. It had been a long day. They ate on the sofa in front of the television. The programme that was just coming on was a magic show. First the screen was full of silver bubbles and then, who should be smiling at them from it but Duggie Bubbles himself.

"Hey, there he is!" said Charlie, speaking with his mouth full and leaning forward excitedly. "He's coming to our Book Bonanza. We're going to see him real, doing his tricks."

Duggie Bubbles had shoulder-length blond hair and a black velvet suit and he smiled all the time. He seemed to be all teeth and smiles. Smilingly, he amazed everyone with lightning card tricks, pulled yards and yards of silk scarves, coloured streamers and live birds out of a top hat and turned a vase of paper flowers into a white rabbit by whisking a cloth over them and tapping them with his little wand.

"It all seems so easy," said Charlie enviously. "It never works like that when I try to do it."

"Looks as though he's going to do a Houdini act now," said Norman.

Still smiling, Duggie Bubbles removed his jacket and allowed himself to be firmly tied up with ropes and shut into a big wooden box, which was secured with more ropes and even chains and padlocks. Everything went dark, with only a spotlight shining down on the box. There was a tense moment of silence. Then a roll of drums, a loud fanfare of music and the lights blazed again as Duggie Bubbles stepped out from behind some curtains, absolutely free! His hair was a little ruffled and he was sweating lightly, but his smile was as broad as ever.

"How does he do it, Norman?" asked Charlie.

"Perhaps there's a hole in the bottom of the box," suggested Norman. But it had already been proved to the viewers that this was not so.

"I'm going to ask him how he does it when I see him," said Charlie.

"Magicians never tell," said Norman.

5 The Magician Appears

The next morning Charlie put on his favourite cap with the big peak and his Superman T-shirt, packed his roller-skates and a couple of cheese sandwiches into his canvas shoulder-bag, and set out for the big hall next to the library. He'd promised to help get the Book Bonanza ready. This probably meant running about and fetching things.

Linda was in command when he got there, and Ariadne was already busy moving piles of books about. Dodger had turned up too, although he hadn't been asked. This was because he often got rather wild and over-excited at Bonanzas. Strictly speaking, he was also on the library black-list for returning some books late and in a nibbled condition. Dodger had insisted that his dog, Prince, had done it. But everybody knew that no pets whatever were allowed in the block of flats where Dodger lived. Dodger's dog was an imaginary one, who followed him about. The real-life Book Nibbler was actually Debbie, Dodger's little sister. But in spite of all this Linda still had rather a soft spot for Dodger, which was why she was letting him be the front legs of the horse. So she sighed and said all right, if he really *was* going to help she supposed he might as well stay.

There were books everywhere, beautiful new shiny ones with brightly coloured covers, being unpacked from boxes all ready for sampling. Ariadne kept getting side-tracked by one she simply had to read and settled down on the floor with it, where people kept tripping over her.

Display stands were arranged all round the hall, and there was a platform at one end with curtains, just like a proper stage. In fact, it *had* once been a stage because long ago the hall had been a theatre. It had a gallery and boxes on either side of the stage where the audience used to sit. Linda had had the good idea of making some book displays in these boxes. One of them was a Haunted House, for mystery stories. The students from the Art College had made some lovely ghosts and bats and other spooky things out of paper, and rows of hairy spiders on strings. Charlie and Dodger were set to work with a pair of steps, hanging up the spiders. They looked great, dangling all around.

"Pass us up some more drawing-pins, Dodger," said Charlie, perched up astride the balcony rail.

Dodger rushed down the steps, tore about looking for the drawing-pin box, and tripped over Ariadne, who happened to be lying under the steps, deep in a ghost story. The steps wobbled and crashed over, leaving Charlie stranded high above their heads.

"Ouch! Watch what you're doing!" yelled Ariadne.

"Hey! Get me down!" shouted Charlie.

"Oh, dear, oh, *dear*!" said Linda.

At this moment, who should appear as though by magic, but Duggie Bubbles himself! The real thing, in person, teeth and all. He looked much the same as he did on television, except that he was wearing a sparkling white suit instead of a black one. He was still smiling.

"Gosh!" gasped Charlie. He swung himself over the side of the rail, hung on to a carved pillar and slid down it to join the others.

"Miss Linda Bowen? I believe you're the organizer?" said Duggie Bubbles, pumping Linda's hand.

"Oh, yes. How do you do? We weren't expecting . . . I mean, this is a lovely surprise." Linda was all pink and flustered.

"I was just passing on my way to the studios so I dropped in to see where you want me to do my act, signing and so forth, and check up on one or two points," Duggie Bubbles went on. "Is this the stage? Small, isn't it? You'll be expecting a big crowd, naturally. I'll be bringing my own equipment and I'll need proper facilities for it, storage and so on. There'll be full press coverage, won't there?"

"Oh yes, I've told the local paper . . ."

"I'd rather imagined that the National Dailies would be in on it. And you'll be laying on television coverage, of course?"

"Well, I . . ."

"I usually like—Good heavens! What are those spiders doing up there?"

"The children were putting them up."

"Oh, I see. Great, kids, great!" For the first time he beamed his smile towards Charlie and Dodger. Ariadne, who was skulking in the background, wasn't included.

"Coming along to have your books signed, are you? Bring your friends—all the fans! Only you'd better have those spiders down when I'm doing my act," he said, turning to Linda again, "rather distracting, you know. Want to get everyone's full attention on me, don't we? Now, if you could just show me the stand where I'm going to sign the books. You've got them all prominently displayed?"

Talking all the while, he allowed himself to be led over to where Linda was arranging a display of all his books.

"It's not quite ready yet, I'm afraid," she apologized.

"Well, that's obvious, dear, isn't it? I see you've got *Magic for Boys and Girls* here, but what about my other book, *Out of My Hat*? The one with the big picture of me on the front?"

"It's ordered. We've got a very good local bookseller here and he'll have it by Saturday, I'm sure."

"It's a particularly good one of me. The fans all like

(42)

that one. You'll see that it's laid on, won't you, there's a good girl." He paused for the first time and glanced round the hall. "Bit chaotic here, isn't it?"

"We've only just started to get it ready this morning. Everyone's working really hard."

"Kids under foot don't help, do they?"

"Children are supposed to be who it's *for*," murmured Linda.

"Will you sign my magic book, please, Mr Bubbles?" asked Charlie, inserting himself into the conversation at this point.

"Afraid I've got to rush now, Sunny Jim," answered Duggie Bubbles, glancing at his watch. "Bring it to the Bonanza and I'll sign it then."

"Are you going to get shut into a box and then get out again, like you did on television?" Dodger asked him.

But Duggie Bubbles was already on his way, disappearing down the hall.

"You'll get all this properly organized by Saturday won't you?" he called back to Linda. "I like my personal appearances to go off properly. And it gives you librarians a chance to do something else except sit about and read books, doesn't it?"

"Goodbye, Mr Bubbles," said Linda politely.

"Nauseating," said Ariadne. "Typical. I might have known it."

"He's ever so good on television," said Charlie. "And he's going to sign my book at the Bonanza, he said so."

6 Stuck in the Mud

"Two very rough-looking men called on me this morning," Uncle Owen Bowen was telling Linda. "Kept asking for Mr Dix. I told them to go over to the barge. Wouldn't let them in, you know. Mr Dix wouldn't like it. Oh dear, no."

"Never mind, Uncle. I don't expect they'll come back," said Linda reassuringly. She was only half listening. Worries about the big Book Bonanza were occupying most of her mind.

They were all eating a sandwich lunch in the little bit of overgrown garden between Uncle Owen's house and the river. It was a welcome break after all the hard work they had done that morning. Uncle Owen had set up his easel by the river wall and was painting the view up towards the bridge. It was low tide. The sun was out, lighting up mirror-like patches of water in the black mud. Mr Dix's barge was moored up high and dry, directly in front of them. It was a smart craft with neat curtains in the port-hole windows and potted geraniums on the deck, more like a bungalow than a boat. Uncle Owen kept glancing anxiously in that direction.

"He's found out about my stove catching fire, you

know," he told them. "Made a terrible fuss about it. Said it was all my fault."

"But I thought he gave it to you in the first place?"

"Says I'm getting forgetful. Smells seem to be getting worse too. And the noises. Sometimes I think I'm starting to imagine things."

"Don't worry, Uncle," said Linda, standing up. "I'm afraid I really must go. There's such a lot to do. Why don't you children stay here? I'll pop back for you at teatime."

Charlie and Dodger thought this was a good idea. They were getting rather tired of helping and wanted to roller-skate on the River Walk. The only trouble was that Dodger hadn't got any skates. He had to take turns with Charlie's. They set off, arguing loudly. Uncle Owen returned to his painting. Ariadne stretched out on the grass nearby with a book. Suddenly the early afternoon peace was broken as Mr Dix banged open his cabin door and strode up on to the deck of his barge. He stood there looking at them with his legs planted well apart, like a captain on a bridge. He was clearly in a bad temper.

"May I ask what you're doing on my private property, Mr Bowen?" he called out. "This garden isn't a public park, you know."

Uncle Owen started guiltily.

"Just doing a little oil painting, Mr Dix. River scene, you know. Such a good light today."

"You have no right to use this garden, Mr Bowen. I've told you before. No lodgers have a right to use the garden. It's in the agreement."

"Sorry, sorry. Always used to paint in this garden. Ever since I've lived here. Very fond of the view, you see."

"People will think I'm running some sort of an art school here," said Mr Dix crossly. "Some sort of hippy colony, with that child lying about all over the grass as though it was her own back yard. And is that the remains of a picnic I can see? Really, Mr Bowen, I must ask you to go, and take her along with you. Right away, if you don't mind."

Uncle Owen did mind. He looked as though he wanted to cry. Mr Dix had really upset him. It was humiliating. With trembling hands he began to pack up his box of paints. Ariadne closed her book. Her lips moved silently to sound her favourite word: "Nauseating!" She stepped forward to help Uncle Owen. His big wooden palette, with its lovely sticky mess of colours still wet, and a fistful of long brushes were lying balanced on the edge of the river wall. While Uncle Owen was fumbling with his easel a spiteful gust of wind whipped up from the river. It blew the canvas face down on to the ground. The easel toppled over and knocked the palette,

and the brushes with it, over the edge. They lay there, stuck down in the river mud between the embankment wall and the barge.

"My palette! My best brushes!"

This was the last straw for Uncle Owen. He sat down on the wall and covered his face with his hands.

"Now look what's happened!" cried Ariadne angrily. "Please, have you got a ladder or something on your barge?" she asked Mr Dix. "The wall's too steep and slippery for me to climb down, and we've got to get them back before the tide comes in!"

But Mr Dix was stonily unsympathetic.

"I'm afraid I can't help you. They'll just have to stay where they are," was all he said.

"But there must be a way of getting down there!" said Ariadne desperately. "I'll run and fetch Charlie and Dodger."

"No. No good," said Uncle Owen wearily. "We'll have to do as Mr Dix says. Leave them where they are. There's no way of reaching them."

"But you won't be able to paint without them!"

Uncle Owen didn't reply. Slowly he began to pick up his canvas and easel from the muddy ground.

At this moment Charlie was swooping like a gull on wheels up at the far end of River Walk, with Dodger running close behind. They were too far away to see what was happening to poor Uncle Owen. But they were not the only roller-skaters out that afternoon. A pair of slithering figures appeared round the corner, at the other end of the walk: two men, one tall and thin with a sly face hunched into his collar, the other tubby and unshaven. They both seemed to be having a lot of difficulty in standing upright. Reeling, clutching one another for support, hanging on to railings and lamp-posts to stop themselves from falling, they edged their way determinedly along.

"Let *go* of me, Trevor. You'll have us both over."

"Terrible idea, this was, Ray."

"Shut up and try to act naturally. We'll get noticed."

At last they reached the railings outside Uncle Owen's front door and hung there, sweating and panting.

"What do we do now then, Trevor?"

The tall man adjusted his beret, clicking his teeth with irritation.

"We skate up and down, Ray, as I told you. Keep our eyes on the barge. Look as though we're enjoying ourselves."

"This isn't doing my weak ankles any good."

"Never mind your weak ankles. Keep skating."

7 Our Mums Wouldn't Like It

Linda had never seen Uncle Owen Bowen so sad as when she returned at teatime. There seemed to be nothing anyone could do to cheer him up. Charlie and Dodger were keen to try and slither down the wall when Mr Dix wasn't about, but Uncle Owen wouldn't hear of it. He said he didn't want them to do anything dangerous. And anyway, how would they ever get up again? There were no steps anywhere near that part of the river. But he had used that palette for years, and brushes were expensive things. Too expensive for an old man to replace easily. He couldn't hide his distress. All the while, from the balcony outside his room at the top of the house, they could see the river tide rising.

It was getting dark. Time for the children to be going home. Kind-hearted Linda, though she was tired, said that she would stay a while and see to Uncle Owen's supper. Ariadne, Charlie and Dodger said goodnight, but they lingered uncertainly outside Uncle Owen's front door. The River Walk was empty. The mysterious roller-skaters were now nowhere to be seen.

"What are we going to do?" said Dodger. "That palette thing and the brushes are going to be washed away when the tide gets to them. And painting pictures is what Mr Bowen really likes doing, isn't it? Just like we like roller-skating. I suppose he's a bit too old for that," he added.

But even Charlie was at a loss for an idea this time.

"I can't stay any longer," Ariadne told them. "*Typical* of my family to be having guests this evening. They'll go on and on at me if I'm not back in time. And I'm late already."

"You'd better go," said Charlie. "Dodger'n me'll think of something." But he didn't sound very confident.

"Pathetic!" muttered Ariadne. And this time she didn't mean Charlie.

Dodger and Charlie hung about in the street after Ariadne had hurried away to catch her bus. They were plunged in gloom.

"Let's have one more look before we go. See how far the tide's come up," Dodger suggested.

"Better make sure Mr Dix doesn't catch us," said Charlie.

Together they slipped quietly through a gap in the railings into the overgrown garden, and crept through the rank undergrowth of brambles and stinging nettles to a vantage point they knew of behind the old shed. From here they could get a good view of Mr Dix's barge without being spotted. The deck of the barge was empty. But light shone from the port-holes of the cabin. Mr Dix was still at home.

Charlie crept silently along in the shadow of the low river wall until he reached the point, just near the gang-

plank of the barge, where Uncle Owen's palette and brushes had fallen.

He peered over the edge. The light was failing, but he could still see them, lying there in the mud. The river was rising fast. Some other barges further up the river were already gently afloat. Charlie looked about him desperately for inspiration. And just at the end of the gang-plank, on the deck of the barge, there it lay: a coiled-up length of rope.

Charlie took his roller-skates out of his canvas shoulder-bag and put them down in the grass. He crept back to Dodger.

"I've got an idea. You'll have to keep watch."

They crept back to the gang-plank. Step by step Charlie edged his way silently along it. The lighted port-holes of the cabin were just below, uncomfortably close. He picked up the rope. But with it he managed to dislodge a pot of geraniums, which rolled over on its side and along the deck. Charlie froze. They both fixed their eyes on the cabin door. But there was only the lapping of the water. After a pause, Charlie came softly back, carrying the rope.

Making it secure was a problem. There didn't seem to be anything to tie it to. If only he'd attended more carefully to all those things they'd told him about knots at Scouts. But Dodger surprised him by having a good idea too. He took one end of the rope right across the garden to the railings and wound it round and round one

of them, securing it with a big
knot of his own invention. It seemed safe
enough. Then he tied another knot at the
other end of the rope, took it across to
the river wall and dropped it over. It was
a longish rope, luckily. The end dangled
just a few feet above the mud.

"Our Mums wouldn't like it if they knew
we were doing this," said Charlie.

"But they won't ever know, will they?"
answered Dodger.

Charlie slung the empty shoulder-bag
over his head, gripped the rope with both
hands and scrambled over the edge. He
swung down, then braced his feet
against the embankment wall like a
rock-climber. He closed his eyes for
a moment, hoping that the railing and
Dodger's knot were as strong as he thought
they were. Then he started to lower
himself down, bumping and slithering
now and again, trying to make as
little noise as possible. He could see
Dodger's white face peering down over
the wall, anxious but reassuring. At
last he reached the bottom of the rope
and dropped the last few feet, landing
ankle-deep in black slime.

Uncle Owen's palette and brushes lay just near his feet. He picked them up and, messy as they were, quickly stuffed them into his shoulder-bag. Now came the really difficult bit. Summoning all his strength, he leapt for the end of the rope. His arms seemed to be being pulled out of their sockets as he spun round, trying to re-establish his foothold on the wall. Then came the climb up, hand over hand.

"Come on, Charlie. You're doing fine!" Dodger whispered to him hoarsely.

The way back seemed endless. His arms were aching terribly. Three quarters of the way he stopped climbing and dangled in space, too tired to go on. He was exactly level with one of the port-holes of Mr Dix's barge. Luckily the light which shone out of it just missed him as he hung there against the wall. But he could see inside quite easily. Mr Dix was at a table, bending over something. He was drawing a picture! Charlie couldn't see his face, or what kind of picture it was. But, propped beside his drawing-board, was something that Charlie recognized at once. It was a small chalk drawing, not in a frame, but unmistakable: The Stunner!

Charlie was shaking all over when, with a final enormous effort, he managed to reach the top of the rope. Dodger's hands gripped his arms and helped him to heave himself over the wall. They both flopped on the ground, Charlie still clutching his shoulder-bag, too tired to move.

"You got them then, Charlie?" whispered Dodger presently.

"Yes, palette and all the brushes, I think," panted Charlie, tipping them out on to the grass.

"Great! Bit messy, aren't they?"

"Mr Bowen won't mind. Hey, Dodger, I saw inside that cabin place. I saw Mr Dix, but he didn't see me. He was drawing . . ."

"Perhaps he's another of these artists," said Dodger, not much interested in this piece of information. "Lucky he didn't look out and see you! Let's go and give these things back to Mr Bowen. He'll be ever so pleased."

"It's getting dark. There isn't time tonight," said Charlie, jumping up and grabbing his roller-skates. "My Mum'll be really mad if I'm not home soon. We'd better hide these things behind the shed. We can get them tomorrow morning and give him a surprise then."

"What about the rope?"

They'd forgotten about the rope. There followed a

terrible struggle to untie it from the railings. Charlie's weight had pulled it tight. At last they managed to wrestle it undone. They didn't want to risk creeping along Mr Dix's gang-plank again, so they left it neatly coiled by the river wall. Then they plunged into the undergrowth to a spot behind the shed, a safe hiding-place for Uncle Owen's precious things.

By now it was getting really late. The slick black water reflected the lights from the barges and the young May moon. Charlie and Dodger squeezed back through the railings and scampered away up the street to their wait-ing suppers. The overgrown garden was full of quiet shadows: two shadows in particular, one long and thin, another squat—Trevor and Ray, no longer pretending to roller-skate, but still watching and waiting. They too had seen what Charlie had seen through the lighted port-hole window.

8 Fishy

When Charlie woke up the next morning his Mum was already busy in the shop, vigorously rubbing up ladies' heads into snowy wigs of white lather. The smell of shampoo came wafting up the stairs. Charlie wondered if she was still cross with him for getting home after dark the night before. She worried about this sort of thing, and worrying always put her in a bad temper. Still, it had been worth it. The first thing Charlie did was to ring up Ariadne and tell her how he and Dodger had got Uncle Owen Bowen's palette and brushes back for him. He made a lot of the dramatic bits, how he had swung like Tarzan over a dizzy drop, which would have meant certain death if he had slipped. Ariadne was furious that she'd missed it.

"And to think I had to spend the whole evening being polite to grown-ups and answering all those questions about how I'm getting on with my 'cello lessons and whether I like my school," she said bitterly. "I couldn't even watch television! It's too nauseatingly pathetic!"

"Meet you at Mr Bowen's house this morning," said Charlie. "We can give him back his things then—give him a nice surprise."

When he rang off he remembered he hadn't mentioned what he had seen through the lighted cabin window. But the thought of it kept buzzing at the back of his mind. It was still bothering him when Norman, who had been working late the night before, emerged for his breakfast. So Charlie told him all about it.

"That Dix character's a bit fishy if you ask me," said Norman, carefully spreading plenty of butter and marmalade on a thick piece of toast. "Linda gets worried about the way he goes on at her uncle all the time. Pretends he's going off his head, which he isn't. Although it would suit old Dix if he did. He can't wait to pack the old man off into a Home so he can move in himself and posh the place up. You can see that a mile off."

"He'd taken that drawing out of its frame, the one of The Stunner, you know, that looks just like Linda."

Norman did know.

"But I didn't know Mr Dix was an artist too. He's never mentioned *that* before. Could you see what he was drawing?" he asked.

"No, he was bending right over it. The Stunner was propped up next to him."

"Fishy," said Norman again, chewing thoughtfully.

"We're going to give Mr Bowen back his things this morning," Charlie told him.

"Think I'll look in there myself. I've got the morning off," said Norman. "Will Linda be there, do you think?" he added casually.

"I don't know. She's busy with the Bonanza. It's

tomorrow, you see!"

When Norman had finished breakfast they went round to River Walk on the motorbike. Ariadne and Dodger met them on Uncle Owen Bowen's doorstep. Together they managed to persuade the old man downstairs and over to the garden.

"It's a surprise," Charlie explained. "We've got your palette and brushes back! Dodger and me rescued them last night before the tide came in."

"Wait there while we get them for you!" said Dodger excitedly.

Uncle Owen Bowen was quite bewildered. He could hardly believe the good news. He stood obediently by the old shed while Charlie and Dodger ferreted about in the nettles.

"We left it just here, I think," whispered Dodger, searching frantically.

"I thought you'd marked the place," said Charlie.

"No, I didn't. It was too dark."

They were getting very scratched and stung. The palette and brushes didn't seem to be where they had left them.

"Come on, Charlie. We're waiting for the surprise," called Ariadne.

"*All right!*" shouted Charlie. He was beginning to get agitated. "It must be somewhere here, Dodger," he hissed.

"Want any help?" said Norman.

Uncle Owen waited eagerly while they all searched. They worked their way right along the back of the shed. With a horrible sinking feeling Charlie began to think that the palette and brushes had disappeared.

"Are you sure you left them here?" Norman asked.

"Course I am." Charlie was in agony. The adventure of the night before and Uncle Owen's surprise seemed to be going all wrong. Already the old man's face was starting to crumple into disappointment, as though this was some kind of cruel practical joke. Norman was kicking the brambles aside. He looked at the muddy ground.

"That's funny," he said. "There's a lot of footprints which look too big to be yours or Dodger's. Somebody else must have been here."

At that moment a whoop of delight came from Dodger.

"Hey, look! They're here!" He was holding up the palette and brushes. "They were in quite a different place to where we left them, all scattered about. I just saw the edge of the palette poking out from the grass underneath this bush, as though someone had thrown them down here."

Uncle Owen was as pleased to see his precious things as though they had given him a hundred pounds. At once he was wreathed in smiles. Filthy as they were he kept fingering them as though he couldn't believe his eyes.

"So *grateful*. So *kind* of you to take the trouble. So *brave*," he kept saying, beaming at Charlie and Dodger. "This must be my lucky day. I thought these were lost for ever, and now I can start another painting. And, do you know, I've got my grandmother's portrait back too! Mr Dix brought her back to me earlier this morning. You must all come up and see her."

Still thanking them enthusiastically, Uncle Owen led them all proudly back to the house and upstairs to his room. There, hanging in her frame in the usual place on his wall, was The Stunner.

9   Very Fishy

"I was *so* pleased to see her again. I missed her almost as much as I did my old palette and my brushes. Now I've got them all back. I just can't believe it!"

"Couldn't Mr Dix sell her then?" asked Norman.

"No, no. Showed it to his friend the expert and, what do you think? He found out that it's a fake! Completely worthless! Not worth more than a few pounds. And all these years I've been thinking it was the real thing. Pre-Raphaelite, you know."

Charlie didn't know. He felt very confused altogether. But Uncle Owen went on happily,

"Of course, my sight isn't what it was. And somehow, you know, I don't really mind a bit. It's a likeness of Lily Bowen, the only one I have, and that's all I care about. I'm glad she isn't valuable. If she had been, I might have been tempted to sell her, you know. And I'd much rather have her here on my wall."

"Well, if you look at it that way, Mr Bowen, I suppose it is a bit of luck," said Norman doubtfully.

Ariadne was silent. But while the others were chatting she stood for a long time in front of The Stunner, peering at her intently.

"I'm glad you've got her back," she said at last.

"The strangest thing of all," Uncle Owen told her, lowering his voice, "is that I've been hearing those noises overhead again. Muffled footsteps. Bangs and thumps. In the evening when there's nobody here, only Beauty and me. It's as though Lily's been trying to tell me something. That she didn't want to be sold at all. That she wanted to come back here with me. Now perhaps she'll stop," he added.

"I hope so," said Ariadne.

Norman said he thought he would go round to the hall and see if he could help Linda with the Book Bonanza, and the children said they'd all come along too. Leaving Uncle Owen happily washing his brushes and rubbing linseed oil lovingly into his palette, they went downstairs. The smells were getting worse. Although the old stove was gone it had left blackened marks on the walls and ceiling, from which bits of old paper hung down in sad festoons. What was left of the carpet was full of holes. A door leading off the hall, down to dark basement regions, lurched drunkenly off its hinges.

"This place is a slum," said Norman, indignantly. "I think Mr Dix is letting it go like this so Mr Bowen will have to move. I keep telling Linda to try and get him to complain to the authorities, but he won't. He's afraid of Mr Dix."

"I wouldn't live here for a million pounds," said Dodger. "My Mum's always going on about the state of the lift in our flats. But she'd have a fit if she saw this. I wonder what's down there?" He peered fearfully down the basement stairs.

"Dare you to go down and see," said Charlie.

"Not likely."

"Go on. I dare you."

"Why don't you go, if you're so brave?" retorted Dodger. At this moment two green eyes appeared in the gloom. They both jumped back hastily. But it was only Beauty, Uncle Owen's old cat. She ran through Charlie's legs, crouched down and regarded them balefully for a moment, and then disappeared upstairs.

Norman went on ahead to the hall on his motorbike, leaving the children to follow on foot.

"You know, there's something very funny going on in that house," said Ariadne as they walked along.

"Mr Dix is acting fishy. Norman said so," said Charlie. And he told her what he had already told Norman, about all he had seen through the port-hole of the lighted cabin the night before.

"He was drawing a *picture*?" said Ariadne. "I thought he was meant to be an art dealer, not an artist."

"Perhaps it's his hobby," said Dodger. "There's going to be a Hobbies competition at the Bonanza tomorrow. A quiz, too, with prizes. I'm going in for everything. The only trouble is," he added, "that I haven't actually got a hobby. But roller-skating's going to be, when I get my new skates. My Dad's going to get me some really good ones. The expensive kind with precision bearings. Much better than your old ones, Charlie."

Dodger's Mum and Dad both had good jobs and earned a lot of money, so Dodger nearly always got the things he wanted. Their flat was stuffed with colour tellys, video cassettes and stereo systems. Even Dodger's little baby sister had her own transistor. But they didn't have time to talk to him much and they never told stories, as Charlie's Mum did sometimes when she was in a good mood. Charlie liked the true ones best, about all the awful things she did when she was a girl.

Ariadne wasn't listening to Dodger. She was thinking hard. She walked more and more slowly, until in the end she stopped altogether.

"I'm going back to Mr Bowen's house," she told them.

"What for?" asked Charlie, surprised.

"Won't be long. See you later," was all Ariadne said, and, before they could stop her, she was hurrying back the way she had come.

(64)

They had closed Uncle
Owen's front door firmly
behind them, as usual,
when they left.

But when Ariadne arrived back at the house she was
surprised to find it slightly open. She walked quietly
inside. The hall was empty. Some instinct stopped her
from calling out. Instead, she tiptoed over to the foot of
the stairs. On the half-landing above her she saw a
kneeling figure, his shadow cast up strongly on to the
peeling wall. It wasn't Uncle Bowen. It was Mr Dix.

There didn't seem anything else for Ariadne to do but
to stand there, watching, unable to go forward or back.
Mr Dix was far too intent on what he was doing to notice
her. He appeared to be burying something under a
floorboard. After a while he stood up and carefully
replaced the board, stamping it into place with his feet.
Ariadne felt as if she was frozen, like the lady in the
Bible who was turned into a pillar of salt, quite unable to
move. Mr Dix was about to turn round. Then their eyes
would meet. Then . . . But when Mr Dix had finished,
he turned the other way without once glancing in her
direction. His footsteps went echoing up the three flights
of stairs to Uncle Owen Bowen's room at the top of the
house. Ariadne could hear their voices, and she could
tell by Mr Dix's tone that he was complaining again.

She crept up on to the half-landing. It was easy to see which was the loose floorboard. She scrabbled at it hurriedly, breaking her fingernails on its rough edges. Now she felt like somebody in a detective story, galvanized into swift action. What had Mr Dix been hiding? Something he didn't want anyone to know he possessed. Jewellery, wads of pound notes, a priceless painting? The floorboard came up. She peered down into the hole, then reeled back on her heels.

What Mr Dix had hidden there was a mouldy kipper!

10 Haunted

Ariadne ran straight round to the hall to tell the others all about her discovery.

"Fishy," remarked Norman.

"It certainly was fishy. It smelt absolutely *nauseating*," Ariadne told him.

"Why should Mr Dix want to put a mouldy kipper under the floorboards of his own house?" Charlie asked. "It smells bad enough in there as it is."

"That's it!" shouted Norman suddenly. "Perhaps he's trying to make the smells *worse*, on purpose, so he'll have a better excuse for getting Mr Bowen out."

"That would be typical," said Ariadne. "I'll bet you're right."

"There was that old stove," Norman went on more thoughtfully, "the one that caught fire. Perhaps Mr Dix put it there specially so it would smoke and give him another excuse to complain. And to think it nearly set the place on fire!"

They all looked at each other, struck silent by such villainy.

"There's something even more fishy I've been wanting to tell you about," said Ariadne at last. "I've been thinking. You know Mr Dix borrowed The Stunner, and now he's given it back to Mr Bowen saying it's a fake, that it isn't worth anything. Not by a famous artist at all, or so his expert friend said. But I had a really good look at it when we were there this morning, and there's something funny about it. It looks different."

"How do you mean, different?" Charlie asked.

"Well, it's really hard to say. But I've looked and looked at The Stunner before—the day when Mr Bowen was telling us all about Lily being a mudlark, you know—and this morning I thought the drawing didn't look the same as it did before. One or two pencil strokes round the edges are different and it's sort of flatter, somehow. You have to look awfully hard to see. Mr Bowen would have noticed himself, of course, but he's a bit absent-minded at the moment."

"He's always forgetting where he's put his glasses," said Dodger.

"I wasn't quite sure. But when you told me, Charlie, about seeing Mr Dix through the port-hole last night, and how odd it was that he had The Stunner propped up beside him when he was drawing, I suddenly thought I wanted to go back and have another look. But I couldn't, because that's when I saw Mr Dix on the stairs."

Charlie and Dodger listened to all this open-mouthed. It was just a bit too difficult to get the hang of all at once.

"Do you mean," said Norman slowly, "that Mr Dix might have been *copying* The Stunner? That he might have given Mr Bowen a fake and kept the real one?"

"Well, he's clever enough to do it," said Ariadne.

"He knows Mr Bowen's sight is bad. Perhaps he thought he'd never notice the difference."

"This is serious," said Norman. "If you're right it's a matter for the police. We must tell Linda about all this. But she's so busy with the Book Bonanza at the moment, I don't want to worry her till it's over. And we can't mention anything to Mr Bowen yet because he gets so anxious and upset, especially about anything to do with Mr Dix. We've got to make sure. We can't go accusing anybody of anything until we've got absolute proof. Now remember, you lot, not a word to anyone for the moment until I can think what to do."

They all promised.

"Fancy all this fuss about a little chalk drawing," Dodger said to Charlie later, as they were humping books about. "My Mum puts all my drawings in the bin."

"You've got to get famous or dead before they're valuable," Charlie told him.

"Well, even if I was both, it won't do me any good if the binman's got them," said Dodger bitterly. "My baby sister usually nibbles them round the edges, too. I don't suppose even that famous artist our teacher was telling us about— you know, the very thin chap, Lean Ardo what's-his-name . . ."

"Da Vinci, I think. The one who tried to invent wings."

"Yes, him. Well, I don't suppose even *he* could have got to be such a famous artist with my Mum and sister around."

"Perhaps he didn't have a Mum, or a sister. Perhaps he could just stay at home all day and paint pictures and invent things."

"Must have been great. Even if he did get thin with nobody to cook his dinners."

That evening, after supper, Norman couldn't settle down to anything. He paced restlessly up and down the sitting-room, frowning deeply and nibbling potato crisps. They helped him to think.

"I'm going for a walk down to the river. Maybe have a chat with Mr Bowen," he said at last.

"Can I come?" asked Charlie promptly.

"It's too late for you to be going out," said Mum, looking sternly round her newspaper. "You've got a big day tomorrow at the Book Bonanza. I'm not having you up till all hours, getting tired out, even if it is half-term."

"But I'm not getting tired out. I'm not in the least bit tired," Charlie protested. "*Please*, Mum. I'll be with Norman."

"We won't be long," Norman said.

Mum wavered for a second and Charlie, taking up the advantage with a skill born of long experience, was already putting on his anorak.

"You've got to be in bed by nine," Mum called out after him as he and Norman ran downstairs.

It was dark now. Down on the River Walk the old-fashioned street-lamps were already lit. There were very few people about, only a few strollers on their way to the pub on the corner. Uncle Owen Bowen's house was shrouded in darkness. Norman and Charlie stood in the street, looking up at his window, but the light was out.

"Must have gone to bed already," said Norman. "We'd better not disturb him. I wanted to get another look at The Stunner but it'll have to wait till tomorrow, I suppose."

They retreated to the other side of the street and leant against the garden railings in the shadow of a straggling elder bush, smelling the night river smells and wondering what to do next. Just then a familiar figure turned the corner and walked briskly up the street towards them—peaked cap, dark glasses, jutting jaw. Mr Dix himself!

Norman and Charlie instinctively drew back into the shadow. Mr Dix hadn't seen them. He stopped under a street-lamp, glancing up at the house. After a moment he felt in his pocket, produced a key, and let himself in.

Norman and Charlie waited and watched. No lights appeared in the windows. The house remained as black and silent as before. After a while they could see a pale light, a torch or a candle perhaps, appearing fitfully on the first floor landing. It disappeared, then reappeared, moving from room to room.

"Is he burying another kipper, do you think?" whispered Charlie. "Why doesn't he put the lights on?"

"Perhaps he doesn't want Mr Bowen to know he's there," answered Norman.

The house went quite dark again. Then, eerily, the light appeared once more, this time in one of the three tiny attic windows above Uncle Owen's room, the attic that was supposed always to be empty. It started to move across the breadth of the house and back again, showing in one window then another. Up and down, up and down, like a ghost walking. Suddenly Mr Dix's profile was thrown up quite sharply against the pane, slightly distorted, like an evil caricature of the man inside. Then the light went out.

Charlie moved closer to Norman. He was very glad that he hadn't come there alone.

"It's scary. Do you think Mr Bowen's awake?"

"No wonder he feels haunted," muttered Norman. "But it's not the ghost of Lily Bowen who's doing the haunting. It's Mr Dix."

"I'd put my head under the blankets if I was in there," said Charlie. But Norman was furiously angry.

"He ought to be had up, frightening an old man like that. It's downright cruel."

"Perhaps he's coming down again," said Charlie. "He'd better not catch us here watching the house."

"Things are fitting together like a jigsaw puzzle," said Norman. "Come on, Charlie, we'd better be going home. I've got to think."

But another piece of the jigsaw, unknown to Norman, was close at hand. They were not the only watchers on the River Walk that night. Two pairs of eyes followed them as they hurried away under the lamplight. Trevor and Ray, crouched in the rank grass of the overgrown garden, stirred stiffly in their hiding place as they watched them out of sight.

11 Dark Doings

"I thought they'd never go," said Ray. "Thought we were stuck here in this blooming grass like a couple of broody swans. Ooo, my leg's gone to sleep."

"Get up, quick. We've got to get going. Wasted enough time as it is," snapped Trevor.

"It's too late, man. Dix is over at the house. He might be back any minute."

"It's our last chance, isn't it? You want to be in on this deal, don't you?"

"Yes, Trevor."

"Well, come *on*, then."

They started to move like two bobbing shadows along the river wall towards the gang-plank of the barge.

"I can't feel my leg at all," whispered Ray, bent double.

"You and your leg. It's always something with you. We wasted all yesterday messing about on those roller-skates with you complaining about your bruises. Then you had to go and sit on that old palette when we were hiding behind the shed and get colours all over the seat of your trousers."

"Wish I hadn't thrown that thing into the bushes now. Might have been worth a bob or two. Brushes too."

"A few bob!" spat Trevor scornfully.

They reached the gang-plank and paused there, eyeing the cabin door. The port-holes were dark. The tide was coming in, and the barge was already lifting on the lapping water. There was no other sound or movement.

"You're sure he's still got the drawing in there?"

"Yeah, sure. We saw him doing the copy, didn't we? And we've been watching him ever since. He hasn't left the barge except to go over to the house. But he's one of the quickest workers in the business. He'll be getting rid of it like a hot potato, tomorrow probably. He's been putting out feelers already, trying to see what kind of price he can get for it from a crooked dealer."

Ray giggled. "You ought to know all about *that*," he said.

"Quick, before he gets here. That cabin door's probably locked but I can get it open in no time. You stay on deck and keep watch."

Trevor hopped silently on to the gang-plank and padded along it like a lean cat. Ray followed, making the boards bend and creak. Together, they were outlined sharply against the sky. Trevor landed lightly on the deck. Ray paused, balancing uneasily.

"You two want something?" said a clear voice suddenly from the bank behind him.

Ray leapt into the air, spun round, and crashed down again with knees bent. The gang-plank groaned. Mr Dix stood there blocking the way. His sun-glasses gleamed menacingly in the darkness like the eyes of a large insect. He seemed to have appeared out of nowhere.

"Gas Board!" cried Ray. "We're from the Gas Board—"

"At this time of night?" Mr Dix took a step forward.

"Just checking. Looking for a leak. Trevor—we've done it wrong again, Trevor—Trevaaaaah . . ."

Trevor reacted more directly. At the sound of Mr Dix's voice he leapt back on to the gang-plank and sprinted along it, cannoning into Ray and throwing him completely off-balance. Locked together, they waltzed wildly. Then Trevor jerked himself free. Reaching the bank, he met Mr Dix head on. For a few dangerous moments they grappled silently.

Ray struggled to keep his footing on the gang-plank, arms out, beating the air like wings. Then he toppled slowly sideways and disappeared from view. A huge splash followed as he hit four feet of water between the barge and the river wall.

Meanwhile Trevor had managed to heave Mr Dix into an elder bush where he collapsed heavily backwards into the headily-scented flowers. Seizing his chance, Trevor tore across the garden and, taking the railings like a hurdler, was away up the deserted street.

"Get him! Stop him, can't you?" roared Mr Dix, but nobody heard. He fought his way out of the bush and began to give chase, shedding white blossoms behind him. Unable to jump the railings, he used some regrettably ugly language as he fumbled with the gate.

By this time Ray had surfaced in the river and was staggering about, spewing dirty water and shouting to Trevor to get him out. But Trevor was already well out of earshot.

Charlie and Norman were on their way home up one of the narrow streets which led away from the river. They heard the cries echoing distantly from River Walk, then swift footsteps running up the street behind them. Norman glanced round, surprised. Then he gripped Charlie's arm.

"Seems to be somebody chasing us. Quick, Charlie. Better be on the safe side. Can you make it to the corner, double quick, do you think?"

Charlie obediently broke into a jog-trot. They could hear Trevor gasping and heaving for breath as he loped up behind them. Norman and Charlie quickened their pace to a run. Trevor was gaining on them. They were nearly at the corner, where the brighter street lights shone, when he drew level with them. Ahead they could see a bus just pulling away from the kerb. Trevor shoved his way violently between them, sending Charlie reeling against the wall, and ran on into the main road. For a moment or two he sprinted level with the moving bus. As it accelerated he put on a desperate spurt and took a flying leap on to the platform. He nearly missed his footing but the conductor caught his arm and hauled him aboard. They saw his white face looking back at them before he disappeared up the stairs.

"*He* was in a bit of a hurry," said Norman. "You all right, Charlie?"

Winded, Charlie was leaning against the wall.

"He didn't half give me a shove," he said, rubbing his elbow. "Worse than the dinner queue at school."

"Must have been his last bus. I'm glad he wasn't chasing us, anyway," said Norman. He took Charlie's arm. "We've got to get you home. Your Mum said nine o'clock, and there'll be terrible trouble if we're late."

But before Charlie could collect himself another flying figure came up the street behind them. It was Ray, oozing water, his clothes flapping desperately about him. He lolloped towards them like a creature risen out of the primeval mud.

"Trevor, wait for me," he was shouting, "Trevaaaah . . ."

Charlie was flung against the wall a second time as he plunged past. Reaching the corner, Ray paused for a moment, moaning, then ran off in the direction of the vanishing bus. Norman helped Charlie to his feet for a second time.

"Nutter night," he said. "They're everywhere. It'll be Things from Outer Space next. Come on, Charl."

They were just turning into the main road when somebody, walking briskly in the other direction, bumped straight into them. For the third time that evening Charlie was nearly knocked off his feet.

"Sorry," said the man briefly, hardly bothering to stop. He didn't recognize Charlie, but Charlie recognized him.

"Hey, Norman, do you know who that was?" he said, staring after him in surprise.

Norman was in no mood for guessing.

"The Incredible Hulk, of course," he said, dragging Charlie forward by the arm. Charlie allowed himself to be dragged, but he was still looking back over his shoulder.

"Didn't you see?" he said excitedly. "It was Duggie Bubbles! I know it was. I saw him quite close up at the hall yesterday. I wonder what he's doing down here?"

"Another disappearing act, probably," answered Norman, striding purposefully homewards.

12 Bonanza Day

Charlie woke up the next morning still thinking about Duggie Bubbles. He had been dreaming that he was sitting on the lid of a box, trying to keep it shut, while Duggie Bubbles, who was inside, kept trying to jump out like a jack-in-the-box. Later in the dream Charlie found himself trying to do magic tricks before a huge audience, but everything he did kept going wrong. Now, fully awake, he remembered it was Bonanza day, and it was late already.

He hurried out of bed and searched about for his favourite book. It was extra large and brightly coloured: *Magic for Boys and Girls*. He was beginning to think that seeing Duggie Bubbles on the way home last night had all been part of his dream. But he was determined to get his book signed at the Bonanza. Mum had told him that signed books were sometimes valuable. He had written his own name already, in bold writing on the fly-leaf: "This Book Belongs to Chas. L. G. Moon." That signature was going to be famous too, he was quite sure.

The first thing he saw when he reached the hall was Ariadne, already encased in her robot suit, walking up and down on the steps in front of the main entrance. She

had a blue light on her head which flashed on and off when she pressed a button inside. The Bonanza hadn't opened yet but already quite a few people had collected and were watching her with curiosity.

"Where's Dodger?" Charlie shouted into one of her small coffee-strainer ears.

"Round the back," came Ariadne's voice, rather muffled, from inside. "He's getting into his half of the horse. Linda's there too. You'd better hurry."

Charlie couldn't resist giving a few raps on her plastic casing. Ariadne flashed her light at him fiercely. Secretly he was rather jealous. Being inside a robot seemed much more fun than the back legs of a horse. He had tried to talk Dodger into letting him be the front part, but it hadn't worked. When Charlie found him in the dressing-room place behind the hall he had already got the head on. The front legs were crumpled round his ankles like concertinas.

"Hee-haw, hee-haw!" he went when he saw Charlie, clattering the huge set of grinning teeth.

"You're a horse, not a donkey," Linda told him. She looked tired and bothered, but pretty, too, in her nice pink dress. "Now be careful with that costume, you boys. The Library Service are having Cuts, so we can't afford to replace it if it gets damaged. Here, Charlie, let me hook you up."

Charlie put down his Magic book in a safe place until later, when Duggie Bubbles was due to arrive. There was a great deal of frantic activity going on all around them. Busy helpers were running in and out, and Linda was answering their questions and giving last-minute instructions as she helped Charlie into his back legs. Once inside, he had to hold on to Dodger's waist firmly. He could see very little, although there were some air-holes so he could breathe.

"For heaven's sake don't go walking backwards," Linda warned Dodger sternly, "and give plenty of warning when you're going to stop."

She fixed large notices on either side of them: "Book Bonanza Today!"

They were off, cantering down the passage, with Dodger whinneying realistically and Charlie behind swishing his tail. The Bonanza had officially begun.

Down on the river, the morning was still and calm. A few seagulls rode the water behind the barge, hoping for breakfast. Mr Dix opened the cabin door a few inches and peered round. Then, having made quite sure that he was not being observed, he locked the door carefully behind him and walked on to the deck. He carried a large book casually under one arm, as though he was planning a morning stroll to the library. He hadn't called the police to report the intruders the night before. He had very special reasons of his own for not doing so. Having chased after Trevor a little way, he had given up and returned to the barge in the hope of cornering Ray. But he was too late. Ray had found a rope-ladder hanging down into the water from another barge a little further up-river. Somehow he had managed to heave himself up it, dodge round the gardens, and make off.

Mr Dix crossed the gang-plank and let himself out through the garden gate. He glanced up and down the street a couple of times, then set off at a leisurely pace. As soon as his footsteps had died away round the corner, two faces slid into view at pavement level, looking after him through the railings of a basement area. Trevor was as foxily alert as ever under his clamped-down beret, but Ray was bleary-eyed and sulky.

They climbed up stealthily to street level and hesitated there for a moment. It was very risky to have come back,

but Trevor had decided to take a last desperate chance. Ray had been against it. He had wanted to stay in bed and nurse his aches after the strenuous events of the night before. Being a burglar didn't suit him. He much preferred a more peaceful way of making a living. He and Trevor ran a dubious Antique shop together, where they sold things which might or might not have been stolen by somebody else. They never tried too hard to find out where they'd come from. Trevor knew just where he could sell a valuable drawing if he could get hold of one. But today it was far too dangerous to try to break into the barge again in broad daylight. So Trevor started off up the street after Mr Dix.

"It'll be all up if he sees us this time," said Ray, hobbling after him. "He'll recognize me for sure and you, too, probably. He'll have us arrested."

"Call the police? You must be joking. He doesn't want to have anything to do with the law, any more than we do." Trevor paused on the corner and peeped round. "Nasty questions. Trouble. The last thing he wants."

"What'll we do if we catch up with him?"

"We're *tailing* him. Just keep out of sight and do as I say."

"I think I've done my back in, Trevor. Felt it go as I hit the water last night."

"So it's your back now, is it?" said Trevor unsympathetically. "What I've ever done to deserve such a useless, gutless, witless partner I don't know. I'd have that drawing by now if I was working on my own."

"I wish you were," said Ray.

A huffy silence followed between them. Lurking in and out of doorways, they followed Mr Dix's progress. Once or twice he glanced back over his shoulder but Trevor managed to keep out of sight, bundling Ray with him. When they reached the busy High Street it became easier not to be spotted, although once or twice they nearly lost sight of him amongst the shoppers. Through a street market and down another side-street, they arrived at the main square. Suddenly Mr Dix seemed to disappear. Anxiously Trevor quickened his pace. Forgetting all caution, he craned his neck above the crowd. Ray caught his arm.

"There he is, Trevor," he said, pointing. "On the steps of the hall over there, where all those flags are. Book Bonanza it says. He's going in there!"

"Come on, then," said Trevor.

13   Horsing Around

Mr Dix was paying his entrance money for the Bonanza when Ariadne clanked past. She was so astonished when she saw him that she nearly dropped her banner. For a moment they came face to face, regarding one another. But Mr Dix was not the kind of person to be amused by an outlandish figure in fancy dress. He pushed on past her into the crowded hall.

Ariadne watched him carefully through her tin visor. He began wandering round the exhibition, stopping now and again to idly flip through a book on one of the stands. Children swarmed everywhere, chatting excitedly, devouring books, collecting badges, filling in quizzes and popping balloons. Ariadne started to make her way round the backs of the stands, pretending she was circling the hall with her banner. She was watching his every move. He strolled round casually in the throng, but he kept glancing about, his dark glasses ranging the hall for something. Or somebody. Once or twice he raised his eyes suddenly from a book and nearly caught Ariadne peering at him from behind the display, but she hurried on, flashing her light innocently.

She noticed that he carried a book under his arm. She

couldn't get near enough to read the title. But when a newly-arrived class of primary school children momentarily surrounded Mr Dix and swept him along in their midst, she managed to jostle near enough to read: *Magic for Boys and Girls* by Duggie Bubbles.

"That's odd," said Ariadne to herself, "very odd. Not at all typical. Oh dear, I wish Norman was here."

Charlie, meanwhile, was already feeling hot and tired inside the back legs of the horse. They had been capering up and down the steps of the hall for some time, displaying their notices and trying to attract the crowds. Dodger, quite carried away with his part, was whinneying gaily, browsing in people's shopping baskets for carrots and gnashing his teeth at them. He caused quite a stir. One little girl even timidly offered him a lump of sugar, which Dodger accepted with a great show, tossing his mane and licking his chops. All this was rather boring for Charlie, who felt that his supporting role of back legs offered no such artistic scope. All he had to do was to hold on to Dodger's belt and go wherever he was led, occasionally kicking out his legs. He was just thinking of suggesting that they have a breather and go to see if there was any free orange drink going in the back room, when they were violently cannoned into by Trevor and Ray, who were running up the steps in a great hurry.

Dodger was caught off-balance and fell back on to Charlie. They sat down heavily, Dodger in Charlie's lap. The two men tripped over both of them. Together they all rolled down several steps on to the pavement.

"Hey, mind my ears!" shouted Dodger, forgetting for the moment that he was supposed to be a horse. Charlie was furious. He couldn't see anything. What was more, this was the fourth time he'd been knocked over in the last twenty-four hours. Blindly he fought his way out from the tangle of limbs. At this moment one of the seams on the horse costume gave way under the strain and Charlie's head popped through, about where the saddle ought to have been. Trevor and Ray stumbled to their feet and ran on up the steps without a backward look. The same two men!

"Those two again!" muttered Charlie, scowling. "They seem to be making a hobby of pushing me over. How many more times are they going to try it?"

"Get your head down," Dodger hissed at him. "You're spoiling everything."

Charlie popped back inside and followed obediently after Dodger as he trotted back up the steps and into the hall in the direction of the back room. They had both had enough of being a horse for the moment. It was certainly time for a breather.

"What are those two doing here, anyway?" wondered Charlie aloud as they were sucking up their orange drink. They were both still wearing their horse's legs while a lady helper was kindly doing some running repairs to the torn seam. Dodger had thankfully removed the head, which sat on the table, grinning amongst the general confusion.

"Perhaps they're following you about," Dodger suggested. "Perhaps they've got up a special club to go about pushing you over. Some boys did that to me once in the school playground. It was awful. But me and my gang fought them off in the end."

"But they didn't even know it was me," said Charlie. "And they don't look like the sort of people who'd be interested in Book Bonanzas. When we get into our costume again let's go and find out what they're doing."

14 Mixed Infant

A puppet show was in full swing. Trevor and Ray were stalking the main hall, keeping well to the side among the ornate pillars. They had already spotted Mr Dix who was still loitering rather aimlessly among the stands.

"What's he want to come in here for?" whispered Ray hoarsely. "It's all kids' books in here." Pausing, he pulled one down from a nearby display. "Fairy-tales! I like those. Giants, witches, princesses and that. I always wanted to be a writer of children's stories you know, Trevor. Just look at these lovely pictures!"

He began to turn the pages with interest until Trevor grabbed the book and thrust it back on the shelf.

"Keep watching Dix," he said irritably. "Don't take your eyes off him."

They began to work their way round behind the stands, still trying to keep Mr Dix in view without being seen. Every so often they passed and repassed Ariadne who was still circling in the opposite direction.

"A robot!" cried Ray, turning to look at her with delight. He seemed to have quite forgotten about his bad back. "Look, Trevor, flashing blue light and all. Clever, isn't it?"

"Reminds me too much of a police car," muttered Trevor, pushing him roughly on.

Charlie and Dodger, back again in their horse costume, were hovering behind them in the shadows.

"What are they doing?" whispered Charlie. It was maddening not to be able to see, and to have to rely on Dodger to tell him everything that was going on. Dodger poked his horse's head round a pillar.

"Just walking round. Seem to be looking for somebody."

"Let's follow them."

They set off at a stately pace, daintily picking up their feet. Ariadne, manoeuvring on the other side of the hall, seemed to be making some kind of signals at them, waving her robot arm frantically. But Dodger couldn't understand what she was pointing at.

The puppet show drew to a close, amid noisy applause. Linda's voice came over the loud-speaker, announcing the next event. The Lady Illustrator had arrived and was going to draw some pictures for the younger children in the smaller room off the main hall. There was a general move in that direction. The spaces round the stands suddenly emptied out. Trevor and Ray were dangerously exposed to view, and, what was worse, Mr Dix seemed to be heading straight for them.

"Quick, Ray, he'll see us. Get out of the way," said Trevor.

They shuffled into a crowd of parents and small children who were filing into the smaller room, where an easel had been arranged with a large piece of blank paper pinned to it. The Lady Illustrator was there already, felt pen in hand.

"Now make yourselves comfortable, everybody," called Linda, who was there to introduce her.

Trevor and Ray lowered themselves uneasily on to cushions on the floor among a drove of toddlers. The grown-ups, perched at the back of the room on chairs and tables, shot them an odd look or two, but the Lady Illustrator started off at once with some bright chat. She was large and artistic-looking, dressed in a colourful tent-like garment and hung about with beads. The effect was of an Indian squaw who was accidentally wearing her own wigwam. She asked the children what they would like her to draw. Some of them were too shy to suggest anything, but after some encouragement the braver ones began to call out some ideas.

"Draw a monster!"

"Draw Red Riding Hood!"

"Draw a wolf!"

The Lady Illustrator worked away obligingly, filling page after page with large felt-pen sketches. Sometimes she paused to answer questions about books and drawing. The children were getting braver and more inventive.

"Draw Rumpelstiltskin!"

"Draw my auntie's budgie!"

"Draw the centre-forward of our team, scoring a lovely goal!"

The Lady Illustrator's hair had begun to escape rather wildly from her bun. The floor was covered with pictures. Ray leant forward with interest. He would have liked to ask her to draw something for him but he knew it would make Trevor cross. A small stir was created at the back of the room as a horse's head appeared inquisitively round the door, but Linda hurried over to it.

"You can't come in here, you two," she whispered. "Go back outside *at once!*"

"What are they doing in there, anyway?" Charlie wanted to know.

"Just Art, that's all," said Dodger.

Now Linda and the Lady Illustrator unrolled a huge piece of paper on the floor. Felt pens were liberally distributed amongst the audience. The Lady Illustrator started to sketch the long shape of a dragon, stretching from head to tail almost the length of the room. Every-

body gathered round and began to join in, filling in the details for themselves. There was a great deal of interested chatter.

"I'm drawing a man with a spear chasing the dragon from behind."

"My man's shooting arrows."

"This is lots and lots of smoke coming out of his mouth . . ."

"And burning flames . . ."

"I'm doing his big pointed teeth."

"Lend us the red a minute, will you?"

"Hang on, I want it for all the dripping blood."

The Lady Illustrator hovered encouragingly, helping the younger ones with a shape here and there. Trevor began to eye the door, shifting restlessly on his cushion. Ray couldn't resist the temptation to pick up a green felt pen and, hoping that Trevor wasn't looking, he carefully began to fill in some neat scales on the dragon's tail.

"We've got to get out of here," muttered Trevor. "For Pete's sake, Ray, stop messing about. We've probably lost Dix by now, and you're acting like a mixed infant."

Ray reluctantly gave up his pen to the little girl next to him, and he and Trevor edged their way towards the door.

Charlie and Dodger were patrolling about outside. Dodger caught sight of them as they slipped out of the door into the main hall. The crowds were denser than ever. Children of all ages, Mums, Dads, Grandpas and Aunties milled happily round the stands, browsing and choosing. Before Trevor and Ray could sight the figure of Mr Dix, there was a commotion over by the main entrance. People were gathering, craning over one another's shoulders. A voice on the loud-speaker announced:

"Your attention, please, everyone. Duggie Bubbles has just arrived! He'll be signing your books at the big stand in the centre of the main hall. Don't miss the Magic Show, which will follow shortly."

Charlie tugged at Dodger's belt.

"Come on, Dodger. Never mind about those two now. We've got to get out of this suit quickly. I want to get my book signed."

15 Smile, Please

The drawing session was over. Willing helpers were clearing up. The Lady Illustrator was being revived with cups of tea. Linda hurried over to welcome Duggie Bubbles and to check for the hundredth time that everything was ready for him on the stand. He was already surrounded by a crowd of children, waving books and bits of paper, and he was signing busily, chatting to reporters from the local paper and flashing porcelain smiles about him, all at the same time.

"Now don't push, children. Just make a little space and wait your turn," said Linda. Organizing a Book Bonanza was even harder work than she had imagined.

Charlie, freed from his role as back legs, shot up to join the queue, clutching his copy of *Magic for Boys and Girls*. Dodger, determined not to be left out of anything, followed close behind. The press of people round Duggie Bubbles was growing all the time and, in spite of Linda's words, there was a certain amount of excited jostling. Charlie found himself being pushed against someone, and nearly fell over for a fifth time with sheer astonishment when he saw who it was: Mr Dix! He turned his dark glasses towards Charlie for a moment, but if he recognized him he had certainly decided to ignore the fact.

"What's *he* doing here?" whispered Dodger from behind. "There seem to be some awfully funny people at this Bonanza."

"*I* don't know. Perhaps he's studying to be a magician, like I am," Charlie whispered back. But he was too busy trying to keep his place in the queue to bother about Mr Dix. He badly wanted to get to Duggie Bubbles and ask him how he did that trick of being tied up in a box and getting out again. He wanted to try it sometime, but he had privately decided not to ask Dodger to be his assistant. Something was bound to go wrong if he did. Mr Dix had somehow managed to push ahead of them. Now he was already thrusting his copy of *Magic for Boys and Girls* into Duggie Bubbles' hands. Charlie, not to be outdone, ducked under his outstretched arm.

"Hold it a minute, Duggie," said a news photographer. "Let's have one of you holding up your books and some of the kids . . . you, with the cap, and you . . . would you mind stepping to one side a moment, sir?"

He pushed Charlie and Dodger into a group with Duggie Bubbles in the centre, holding up two copies of *Magic for Boys and Girls*, one in either hand.

"Let's have a big smile, now!" said the photographer.

The camera flashed. Mr Dix skulked in the background, his jaw set angrily.

"Hey, Charlie, we're going to be in the newspaper!" said Dodger, all agog.

"About that trick, the one where you get shut in the box," Charlie began. "Please can you tell me . . ."

But Duggie Bubbles didn't seem to be listening. He was still smiling and signing, but his face was half turned towards Mr Dix. They exchanged a few quick words over Charlie's head. Then the crowd pressed forward impatiently and Charlie's chance was lost.

"There were lots of things that I wanted to ask him about, and now I'll never find out," Charlie grumbled to Dodger when he found himself pushed out to the edge of the crowd again, with his book under his arm.

"Typical!" commented a voice from behind them. It was Ariadne of course. She was still wearing her robot suit, but she had propped her banner up against a pillar and was watching events from the side of the hall. "There are some fishy things going on at this Bonanza, Charlie, if you ask me. I've been following Mr Dix around for ages but I still can't make out what he's doing here. He certainly doesn't seem much interested in the books."

"And we've been trying to track two *very* fishy characters who keep pushing me over," said Charlie. "Only we've lost them now," he added.

"Pathetic!" said Ariadne. "Oh, dear. I can't think what we ought to do now. It's awfully bad for my brain being inside this robot suit. If only Norman was here."

"He is," said Dodger. "Look, over there."

"Thank *goodness*," said Ariadne with relief. They all hurried over to where Norman was examining a pop-up book with great interest.

"Got off early from work," he told them. "Thought I'd come along and see what's happening. Where's Linda?"

All three children started to talk at once, each telling him something different. But their voices were drowned by another announcement on the loud-speaker:

"The Duggie Bubbles Magic Show will begin in five minutes on the stage at the end of the main hall. Take your places, please."

"Come on, let's try and get near the stage," said Charlie, dragging Norman's arm. "We'll tell you everything later. I want to watch all the tricks from really close up so I can see how he does it."

There was a rush for seats. There weren't enough for everyone. Charlie nimbly threaded his way through the crowd and just managed to bag a place in the second row. Dodger immediately plumped himself down in the row behind him, but Norman and Ariadne were somehow left behind.

"Where are they?" said Charlie, craning his neck. "I hope they don't get left in the standing-room-only."

There was a buzz of excitement all about them. Some helpers were setting up the stage for Duggie Bubbles' act. There was a small table with a fringed cloth, some screens and a trolley with all sorts of strange objects on it. On either side of the stage there were displays with huge posters of Duggie Bubbles' larger-than-life-size smiling face and many copies of *Magic for Boys and Girls*.

"Let's see where he's written his name in your book," said Dodger, leaning over the back of Charlie's seat. Charlie opened his copy at the front page.

"I've been fiddled!" he cried furiously. "This isn't my book! Look, it's got Duggie's signature in it all right, but it hasn't got mine. I wrote it in specially, 'This Book Belongs to Chas. L. G. Moon'. I've got the wrong book!"

"Well, it looks much better than your old one, anyway," said Dodger. "Yours had all that marmalade and tomato ketchup spilt on it. Hey, when's this show going to begin?" He stood up in his seat, trying to catch a glimpse of Duggie Bubbles in the wings.

"But I don't *want* this one," muttered Charlie indignantly, flicking through the pages. "I *liked* my old one. What's this, then?"

He had come across a loose leaf of paper, concealed between two of the pages. It was just smaller than the size of the book, quite thin, and overlaid with a sheet of tissue paper. Charlie folded it back. A face looked up at him that he knew well, a very pretty face, framed with long curly hair: The Stunner.

16 Black Magic

Ariadne had been separated from Norman in the rush for seats. She was trying to make her way among those people who were standing at the side of the hall, to get nearer to the stage, when a burst of applause greeted the appearance of Duggie Bubbles himself. He launched at once into a flow of jokes and patter, at the same time doing some astonishing things with playing-cards, shuffling them with the greatest skill, picking aces out of his ears, his hair, and what seemed like empty air. He followed with a rapid succession of tricks with coloured balls (which appeared from some equally extraordinary places), and tossed a silk cloth over a transistor, which was blaring out military marches at full blast, and threw the whole thing into the air, making the set disappear

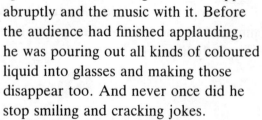

abruptly and the music with it. Before the audience had finished applauding, he was pouring out all kinds of coloured liquid into glasses and making those disappear too. And never once did he stop smiling and cracking jokes.

Then came the familiar empty top hat from which he began to pull

yards and yards of multi-coloured
silk handkerchiefs, paper
flowers, strings of sausages, miles
of streamers, and, finally, two snow-
white live doves. One of them strutted,
cooing, across the stage. The other
fluttered up to the rail of one of
the old theatre boxes and perched there,
calmly preening its feathers.

The audience were all intent on
Duggie Bubbles as he started yet another
trick. He was keeping them all laughing.
But Ariadne was looking up. Behind
the curtains of the box she had
caught sight of something. A man's
figure was standing there, half hidden
in the shadows. When he moved slightly,
the glasses gleamed. Mr Dix, like a
Demon King waiting in the wings, was
staring down at the stage.

Ariadne tried to attract Norman's attention. She could see him over the tops of people's heads, standing next to Linda, but she couldn't get near them. Every time she tried to wave, her suit made a noise like a binful of old tin cans.

"I've just got to get out of this thing," said Ariadne to herself. She edged her way over to the exit and set off down the corridor to the small untidy helpers' room behind the stage.

Ariadne was not the only person who had seen Mr Dix up there. Trevor and Ray, in a dark corner beside the display of posters, were still hot on his trail.

"There he is!" whispered Trevor.

"Where?" said Ray, gazing about him.

"Shhhh, shhhh!" said all the people round about.

Trevor was already pushing his way through them towards a side exit.

"I can't think why we're *bothering*," said Ray, lowering his voice to a piercing whisper as he struggled behind. "He's probably flogged that drawing by now."

"*Would* you mind being quiet?" said a lady threateningly.

Up on the stage Duggie Bubbles was saying, "Now, I'm going to ask a member of the audience to step up here. Don't be shy, now—any boy or girl—what about you, young man? Would you come up and give me a hand?"

"He means you," said Dodger, giving Charlie a shove from behind.

"What?" said Charlie, startled.

"That's right," said Duggie. "The young man in the red cap. We've met before this afternoon, haven't we? Bring your book with you."

Bewildered, and clutching the copy of *Magic for Boys and Girls* with The Stunner still between the pages, Charlie found himself being helped up the steps and on to the stage. Beaming, Duggie Bubbles was pumping him by the hand.

"Now, what's your name? Charlie? This is Charlie, everyone! Give him a big hand now!"

Charlie smiled foolishly as everybody clapped, but the clapping soon turned to laughter as, when Duggie released his hand, he found himself holding an egg. It seemed to have appeared out of nowhere. He was even more surprised when Duggie pulled another one out of his left ear. And before he could wonder how it got there Duggie said,

"Would you mind lending me your handkerchief? I've got a shocking cold," and he began to pull one coloured silk handkerchief after another out of Charlie's back pocket.

Charlie stood there with the book under his arm, blinking with amazement. Things were happening too quickly. The events of the last few minutes seemed unreal, as though he had truly been bewitched. Only Dodger's face, open-mouthed, in the audience below, seemed to make sense.

Mr Dix had shrunk back into the shadows of the box. Quietly he opened the door at the back and slipped out. He paused at the top of the flight of stairs which led down to the corridor below, listening. There seemed to be nobody about. Everyone was watching the show. Gales of laughter came from the hall as Duggie Bubbles pulled more and more extraordinary things out of Charlie's pockets. Suddenly Mr Dix heard footsteps running along the corridor and up the stairs towards him. As they drew nearer he heard a voice saying,

"I think I ought to go home, Trevor. Sitting on that floor hasn't done my back any good, you know—"

Trevor and Ray came round the turn in the stairs and they all met face to face. Mr Dix recognized them both instantly. He towered above them, dark with rage.

"You! Following me about, are you? Spying on me, eh? Tried to break into my barge last night, didn't you? Well, I'm going to settle you two, once and for all!"

But Trevor and Ray had already turned in their tracks like lightning and were scrambling back down the stairs the way they had come. With Mr Dix after them, they swerved into the corridor and tore off towards the helpers' room at the other end. Ariadne was just coming out. They cannoned into each other head on.

"Quick, Ray!" gasped Trevor, pushing her roughly out of the way. He wrenched open a small door on his right and both men tumbled down the dark flight of steps which led into the space under the stage. Ariadne flattened herself against the wall as Mr Dix rushed past in hot pursuit. He disappeared after them like an angry ferret down a rabbit-hole.

Ariadne tip-toed to the door and peered after them into the darkness below. The sounds of a struggle had broken out. She could hear them scuffling and blundering about.

"Typical!" she commented under her breath.

Meanwhile, on the stage above, Duggie Bubbles had taken the book from under Charlie's arm and was holding it up to the audience.

"Here it is, folks: *Magic for Boys and Girls*! All the secrets of wizardry and illusion! Let me show you . . ."

Before Charlie could stop him, he began to turn the pages. As he did so clouds of confetti flew out and drifted like snow across the stage.

"There's plenty of good card tricks in here," said Duggie, as, from another opening, he drew out four aces, "but you have to be very careful about taking this magic book up to bed with you at night, you know, Charlie, very, very careful indeed."

Out of the book came a folded piece of paper. Duggie shook it open. It was not, as Charlie had expected, The Stunner, but a huge concertina of black tissue paper on which was painted a grinning skeleton with gangling arms and legs.

The thumps and bumps that were going on under the stage were drowned in applause as Duggie handed the book back to Charlie, and he made his way back to his seat.

"How on earth did he do it?" said Dodger, awe-struck. "I was watching him all the time and I never saw him put all those things in between the pages."

But Charlie didn't answer. He was searching through the book, page by page. Suddenly he leapt to his feet with a wild shout, as though he'd been scalded. The Stunner had disappeared!

"Sit *down*! We can't see!" chorused the children in the row behind.

But Charlie wouldn't sit down. This was all just too much. He felt as though he was going to burst. Scarlet in the face, he stormed back up the steps and on to the stage, stopping Duggie Bubbles dead in mid-patter.

"The drawing! Where's that drawing?" shouted Charlie. He was so furious he felt like a giant. The very boards seemed to be trembling under his feet. The audience, thinking that this was all part of the show, clapped him good-humouredly.

The commotion under the stage was getting louder. The boards were trembling all right, as Trevor and Ray crashed about in the dark beneath, grappling grimly with

Mr Dix. Just then Ray struck out with a wild swinging blow, missed, and fell flat on his face, bringing Mr Dix down with him. Trevor staggered against them, clutching at a wooden lever for support. It gave way. There was a strange clanking noise and a groaning of old boards. A trap-door in the stage above swung open, and Duggie Bubbles disappeared abruptly from view. Charlie found himself alone on the stage, staring down at a heap of wildly waving arms and legs in the pit which had opened at his feet.

17 A Game of Grandmother's Footsteps

The audience loved it. They clapped loudly. It seemed like the perfect ending to a Magic Show for the Magician himself to disappear. This was even better than television.

"Something's gone terribly wrong!" gasped Linda, clutching Norman's arm. Together they hurried out of a side exit and ran to the door which led down under the stage. There they met Ariadne, still peering down the steps with some interest.

"A big fight," she told them briefly, "Mr Dix and two other men. And I think there's someone else in there now, but I can't think how he got there. It's too dark to see who's winning."

The sounds of struggle and terrible oaths which came from below were getting louder and louder. At last one figure broke free and lumbered up the steps. It was Ray. He was wild-eyed, his sleeve was ripped, and he was covered in cobwebs and grime. Closely on his heels followed Trevor, in a similar sorry state. One after another they pushed past the little group at the top of the steps and ran off at full speed in the direction of the main exit. A third figure staggered out after them. Without his

cap or his dark glasses, Mr Dix was almost unrecognizable. He was very nearly bald and his eyes seemed nakedly small and deep-set, like those of an angry gorilla. His teeth were bared in a snarl of rage. He didn't look in the least like his usual self, but, for a split second, Ariadne thought he seemed oddly familiar. He gave them all a furious, lowering look before pursuing Trevor and Ray down the corridor at amazing speed.

"Are you all right, Mr Bubbles?" called Linda anxiously from the top of the steps.

"What do *you* think?" answered a hollow voice from the gloom below.

In the hall above the audience were still applauding, half hoping for an encore. When none was forthcoming they began to drift happily away. It had all been a huge success. They had never expected, when they paid their entrance money, that the Book Bonanza was going to be quite such a lively event as this.

Charlie stood hesitating on the stage, all his anger suddenly deflated. Too many weird things had happened all at once. He felt so bewildered he was ready to cry. He had even begun to wonder if he really had found The Stunner's picture inside that book, or if he'd imagined the whole thing. Dodger scrambled up on the stage to join him.

"That last bit was great, wasn't it?" he said, peering down the trap-door. "I never expected him to do that."

Down below Linda and Norman were helping Duggie Bubbles up the steps and leading him away to the helpers' room at the back of the stage. Luckily he was more or less unhurt. Landing on top of Ray had cushioned his fall. Linda apologized over and over again, and flustered helpers rushed for cups of tea and brandy.

Dodger wandered curiously about the stage. He peered into Duggie Bubbles' top hat and cautiously touched one or two other props, half afraid that some magic might suddenly rise up out of them and take him unawares. But Charlie hadn't the heart to investigate. He had decided in the last half hour that he didn't want to be a conjuror any more. Making magic was altogether too difficult, and, even if you could make it, still harder to control. And being on stage with a real magician hadn't been any fun at all. It had just made him feel foolish. He wandered off across the stage, miserably kicking up some bits of confetti which were still lying there.

"Hey, look, Charlie!" called Dodger. "Here's that skeleton thing that he pulled out of the book!" And he jerked the paper concertina open with a flourish. Some-

thing fell out of it and drifted across the stage, coming to rest at Charlie's feet. He picked it up. Then he let out a yell of triumph.

"It's The Stunner!" he shouted. "I was right! He *did* take it after all!"

"Not that drawing again," said Dodger. "I just can't understand why everyone goes on about that silly old drawing."

All the same, he followed Charlie as he rushed off to the helpers' room to find Norman, waving The Stunner. Linda, Norman and Ariadne were hovering attentively about Duggie Bubbles, who was slumped in an armchair. He wasn't smiling any more. His eyes popped and his jaw hung slackly, making him look more like a discarded ventriloquist's dummy than a magician.

"Here's The Stunner . . ." began Charlie breathlessly. "Got her back . . . found her in my Magic book . . . only it turned out not to be my Magic book after all . . . couldn't tell you, Norman, because then I had to go up on the stage and be magicked at myself . . . and when I got off it again, it wasn't there, you see, and so . . ."

Nobody was listening to this explanation, even if they could have followed half of what Charlie was trying to tell them. They were all staring at The Stunner. Ariadne was the first to recover from her surprise. She took the drawing out of Charlie's hand and looked at it carefully.

"I think it's The Stunner, all right, the real one," she said. "I *am* glad to see her again."

"We've just found it, up on the stage," Charlie explained. "Inside that skeleton thing."

Now they all turned to Duggie Bubbles. His expression was blank. He was the only one among them who had showed no surprise at Charlie's dramatic entrance.

"I never wanted it," he said. "Didn't want anything to do with it. Never saw the wretched thing until today."

"It's Linda's uncle's drawing," said Norman quietly, "and apart from being valuable, it's very precious to him for family reasons. At the moment he still hasn't realized that he's been robbed of it, because there's a clever fake hanging on his wall in its place, put there by Mr Dix. We couldn't tell you, Linda, until after the Bonanza was over. We didn't want to worry you, and anyway, we weren't sure. But now perhaps you'd like to explain, Mr Bubbles, what it's doing here."

Duggie Bubbles' face had lost all its doll-like pink colour. He looked suddenly grey, and years older.

"It'll be the end of my career if this goes any further. I'll be finished if the papers get hold of it . . ." His voice trailed away miserably. They waited. "You see," he said, "Duggie Bubbles is my stage name. My real name's Douglas Dix. Howard—that's Mr Dix—is my older brother."

"I *thought* there was something familiar about him when I saw him without his dark glasses!" said Ariadne.

"I don't see him very often. We've never got on well. He's a lot older than me, and I don't like some of the ways he has of making money," Duggie told them. "Anyway, being seen about with him wouldn't have been very good for my image. But he rang me up out of the blue the other day and said he wanted me to keep something for him. For safety, he said. A small drawing. Said there were some people he didn't trust watching the barge, and he had to get rid of it as soon as possible."

"Why didn't he ring the police?"

"Oh, he'd never do that. He doesn't like to involve the police for, er, personal reasons. I didn't like it at all. But he puts a lot of pressure on. Says he knows things about me that would ruin my career. So I said I'd go down to the barge and collect it from him. Last night, that was. But when I got near to the river there seemed to be a spot of trouble going on. Some sort of fight. So I beat it as fast as I could. You can't afford trouble in show business, you know."

"We were there too," put in Charlie, "I saw you. Do you remember, Norman? And those two men, the ones that kept pushing me over. They were here today, at the Bonanza."

"They must have been the same two who were watching the barge. They must have been after The Stunner too," said Norman.

"Probably," Duggie agreed. "My brother telephoned me again early this morning. Sounded pretty anxious.

Said he was being watched all the time, but that he was going to get to the Book Bonanza somehow—he knew I was making a personal appearance there—and smuggle the drawing to me in a copy of my book. He wanted me to hang on to it for him until the coast was clear."

"So *that's* what Mr Dix was doing at the Bonanza," said Ariadne. "I followed him all afternoon, but I never guessed he had The Stunner inside that book."

"And we were following those two men, who were following Mr Dix . . ." said Charlie.

"Until he turned round and caught them at it. Just like a game of Grandmother's Footsteps!" finished Ariadne.

"I thought I'd let Howard slip me the drawing," Duggie continued, "but I didn't want to have anything to do with stolen goods. I was going to make him give it back, or return it myself if I could find out who it belonged to. I would even have gone to the police, even if he is my brother. But when I got hold of the book, the drawing wasn't inside. It was the wrong copy. They must have got muddled up when the news photographer was taking the picture. We realized that as soon as we looked inside and saw this kid's name."

"Chas. L. G. Moon," Charlie prompted him.

"Howard was furious. I've never seen him in such a rage. He threatened to ruin my act. So I had you up on stage and got it back."

"But how did you do it?" Dodger wanted to know. "I was watching you every second."

But Duggie Bubbles wasn't telling him that.

"I'm a magician, aren't I?" was all he said.

18 Escape!

Trevor and Ray had reached the River Walk, pouring sweat and sobbing for breath, but still running. Twice they had nearly managed to throw Mr Dix off the scent, skidding round corners, dodging down side-roads, running the wrong way up one-way streets, scattering shoppers at every turn. But he had clung on relentlessly. Though he was the older man by far, rage seemed to fire his pace.

"Oooh, my back! My legs! My weak ankles!" cried Ray piteously as he puffed behind Trevor, but Trevor didn't seem to hear. He was making for a small wooden landing-stage which stuck out from the river embankment between two moored barges. A ladder led down to the water, where a small boat, which belonged to one of them, was tied up. Mr Dix was gaining on them rapidly. They scrambled over a low wall, and across somebody's garden, recklessly treading down the plants. They had reached the landing-stage when Mr Dix caught up with them. Trevor was already half-way down the ladder. Ray was hopping about on the platform above. His shoe had come off. A split second before Mr Dix made a grab at him, he picked it up and hurled it. It caught Mr Dix a

stinging blow on the side of his head. He staggered about, cursing.

"Wait for me, Trevor!" Ray's voice was a high-pitched scream.

He slithered down the ladder and gave a great leap into the boat. It rocked dangerously as he landed in it, nearly capsized, but not quite. It turned round twice, quite out of control, drifting away from the landing-stage. They had no oars. Trevor, hunched in the bows, was paddling with his hands for all he was worth. Ray lay flat on his back in the bottom of the boat, moaning.

"Paddle, Ray, you daft idiot, for pity's sake, paddle!" shouted Trevor.

The boat drifted out a little way and seemed to waver uncertainly. Ray dragged himself up over the side and flapped a hand hopelessly in the water. His weight listed the boat over to one side. It spun round once more. Then, quite suddenly, a swift current caught it and they were carried out into the main course of the river, away on the out-going tide.

Mr Dix was forced to stand there and watch them go. He couldn't contain his fury. Lifting his arms to heaven, he let out a wild cry. He shook his fists in the air. He literally capered with rage. But his foot caught against Ray's discarded shoe. He staggered for a moment, then tipped headlong over the edge of the landing-stage into the river below. Great ripples marked his fall. When at last his dripping head emerged from the filthy water, he was just in time to hear Ray's voice, carrying faintly back over the tide,

"This isn't doing my rheumatism any good, you know, Trevor . . ."

19 A Little Celebration

A few days later, a little celebration was about to take place at Uncle Owen Bowen's. His room had been slightly tidied up and the table was laid with all sorts of delicious food: egg sandwiches, sausage rolls, plenty of chocolate biscuits and a big fruit cake with nuts and cherries on top. There was fizzy lemonade and even a bottle of wine for Uncle Owen himself. Linda had taken him for a stroll by the river. This was supposed to be so the children could get everything ready, but it was really so that Norman could have time to return The Stunner to her original frame and rehang her on the wall without Uncle Owen ever knowing the difference.

"But *why* can't we tell him?" Charlie wanted to know. "It was so exciting about Duggie Bubbles disappearing through the stage and me finding her and everything."

"People as old as Mr Bowen aren't as fond of excitement as you are," Norman told him. "They like a more peaceful kind of life. It's all thanks to you we got her back for him, Charlie. And we'd never have found out what was going on here if it hadn't been for you, Ariadne, and Dodger too. But Linda thinks it's better if he never knows about The Stunner being taken from him. It would only upset him. But we'll have to see that he doesn't let her out of his hands again."

"But what about Mr Dix?" asked Charlie.

"Vanished. Scarpered. Completely disappeared. Or so Linda's just been telling me," said Norman, working away busily. "Nobody's seen him since the day of the Bonanza. I think that magician brother of his, Duggie Bubbles, has told him to get out of London quickly, before there's trouble. Or he might have decided for himself that things were getting too hot for him. He must know by now that he's lost all hope of getting The Stunner for himself, and, what's more, we could have the law on him for forgery if he shows his face here again."

"What are you going to do with that copy?" Ariadne wanted to know.

"Put it in a package and post it through the letter-box of his barge, I suppose," answered Norman. "It's all locked up and empty there, Linda says. Only a few empty milk bottles left on the gang-plank." He carefully straightened the real Stunner in her frame on the wall and stood back to admire his handywork. "Lovely, isn't she?" he said, but he was looking over at the door, where Linda had just appeared, rosy-cheeked and looking rather stunning herself, with Uncle Owen following close behind. He beamed with pleasure at the sight of the loaded table.

"A party! How *kind* of you all. I love parties. Used to go to a lot of them at one time. What a wonderful cake! When can we start?"

(123)

As all the chairs were occupied by stacks of paintings, they began at once, without bothering to sit down.

"A very curious thing about Mr Dix," said Uncle Owen, munching away happily. "Nobody can understand why he left so suddenly. Overnight, without a word, not even to me! A neighbour of mine said she saw him running down the River Walk, dripping wet and shouting, but that must be just wild gossip, of course. Extraordinary fellow. But, do you know, the people from the Welfare Service have been round to see me, and they say I can stay here as long as I like! And, I must admit, it's lovely here without Mr Dix. I can paint down by the river whenever I want to now. Quite like old times. Beauty thinks so too, don't you?" He bent down to offer a piece of roll to the old cat who was purring about his legs.

"Linda and I'll decorate the hall for you when we've got some time off, if you like," Norman offered.

"You're too kind, too kind. Do you know, the whole house has changed since Mr Dix went away? Even the smells seem to have disappeared. And I never hear those footsteps overhead at night any more. I really think Lily must be quite at rest at last."

They all looked at The Stunner. A pale rippling light was thrown up from the river on to the wall where she hung. Even Dodger stopped short, with a chocolate biscuit half-way to his mouth, and gazed at her, as though he'd just caught sight of her for the first time.

"I *think* I see why you were making all that fuss," he said at last, through a mouthful of crumbs, "about her being pinch—" but here Charlie nudged him warningly in the ribs with his elbow, "—about her hanging there," he corrected himself quickly. "She does look rather a pretty kind of lady."

"Not half bad," agreed Norman.

"Beautiful," said Ariadne. "I'm so glad she's yours, Mr Bowen."

"She's only mine in a way," said Uncle Owen, filling his glass. "Art belongs to everyone, really, you know. Especially to you young people—to you, Ariadne, my dear, and Charlie and Dodger here. It gets handed on from us older people to you young ones because it *belongs* to you. It's not something chilly or stuck-up or always in a glass case. It changes all the time. And it's not only painting, it's singing and dancing and books and libraries and telling stories and acting plays and getting a good tune out of a musical instrument. It's yours by right, and it's worth sticking up for and never letting anyone take away from you. Because it's the best present you'll ever have."

"Here's to Art, then," said Norman, raising his glass.

"And here's to *you*, Mr Bowen," said Charlie Moon.

TITLES IN THE NEW WINDMILL SERIES

Chinua Achebe: *Things Fall Apart*
Louisa M. Alcott: *Little Women*
Elizabeth Allen: *Deitz and Denny*
Eric Allen: *The Latchkey Children*
Margery Allingham: *The Tiger in the Smoke*
Michael Anthony: *The Year in San Fernando*
Bernard Ashley: *A Kind of Wild Justice*
Enid Bagnold: *National Velvet*
Martin Ballard: *Dockie*
Stan Barstow: *Joby*
H. Mortimer Batten: *The Singing Forest*
Nina Bawden: *On the Run; The Witch's Daughter; A Handful of Thieves; Carrie's War; Rebel on a Rock; The Robbers; Devil by the Sea*
Rex Benedict: *Last Stand at Goodbye Gulch*
Phyllis Bentley: *The Adventures of Tom Leigh*
Paul Berna: *Flood Warning*
Judy Blume: *It's Not the End of the World; Tiger Eyes*
Pierre Boulle: *The Bridge on the River Kwai*
E. R. Braithwaite: *To Sir, With Love*
D. K. Broster: *The Gleam in the North*
F. Hodgson Burnett: *The Secret Garden*
Helen Bush: *Mary Anning's Treasures*
Betsy Byars: *The Midnight Fox*
A. Calder-Marshall: *The Man from Devil's Island*
John Caldwell: *Desperate Voyage*
Ian Cameron: *The Island at the Top of the World*
Albert Camus: *The Outsider*
Victor Canning: *The Runaways; Flight of the Grey Goose*
Charles Chaplin: *My Early Years*
John Christopher: *The Guardians; The Lotus Caves; Empty World*
Richard Church: *The Cave; Over the Bridge; The White Doe*
Colette: *My Mother's House*
Alexander Cordell: *The Traitor Within*
Margaret Craven: *I Heard the Owl Call my Name*
Roald Dahl: *Danny, The Champion of the World; The Wonderful Story of Henry Sugar; George's Marvellous Medicine; The BFG*
Andrew Davies: *Conrad's War*
Meindert deJong: *The Wheel on the School*
Peter Dickinson: *The Gift; Annerton Pit*
Eleanor Doorly: *The Radium Woman; The Microbe Man; The Insect Man*
Gerald Durrell: *Three Singles to Adventure; The Drunken Forest; Encounters with Animals*
Elizabeth Enright: *The Saturdays*
J. M. Falkner: *Moonfleet*
Jane Gardam: *The Hollow Land*
Leon Garfield: *Six Apprentices*
Eve Garnett: *The Family from One End Street; Further Adventures of the Family from One End Street*
G. M. Glaskin: *A Waltz through the Hills*
Rumer Godden: *Black Narcissus*
Kenneth Grahame: *The Wind in the Willows*
Graham Greene: *The Third Man* and *The Fallen Idol*
Grey Owl: *Sajo and her Beaver People*
John Griffin: *Skulker Wheat and Other Stories*
G. and W. Grossmith: *The Diary of a Nobody*
René Guillot: *Kpo the Leopard*
Thomas Hardy: *The Withered Arm and Other Wessex Tales*
Ann Harries: *The Sound of the Gora*
Jan De Hartog: *The Lost Sea*

Erik Haugaard: *The Little Fishes*
Esther Hautzig: *The Endless Steppe*
Bessie Head: *When Rain Clouds Gather*
Ernest Hemingway: *The Old Man and the Sea*
John Hersey: *A Single Pebble*
Nigel Hinton: *Getting Free; Buddy*
Alfred Hitchcock: *Sinister Spies*
C. Walter Hodges: *The Overland Launch*
Richard Hough: *Razor Eyes*
Geoffrey Household: *Rogue Male; A Rough Shoot; Prisoner of the Indies; Escape into Daylight*
Fred Hoyle: *The Black Cloud*
Shirley Hughes: *Here Comes Charlie Moon*
Henry James: *Washington Square*
Josephine Kamm: *Young Mother; Out of Step; Where Do We Go From Here?; The Starting Point*
Erich Kästner: *Emil and the Detectives; Lottie and Lisa*
M. E. Kerr: *Dinky Hocker Shoots Smack!; Gentlehands*
Clive King: *Me and My Million*
John Knowles: *A Separate Peace*
Marghanita Laski: *Little Boy Lost*
D. H. Lawrence: *Sea and Sardinia; The Fox* and *The Virgin and the Gypsy; Selected Tales*
Harper Lee: *To Kill a Mockingbird*
Laurie Lee: *As I Walked Out One Mid-Summer Morning*
Ursula Le Guin: *A Wizard of Earthsea; The Tombs of Atuan; The Farthest Shore; A Very Long Way from Anywhere Else*
Doris Lessing: *The Grass is Singing*
C. Day Lewis: *The Otterbury Incident*
Lorna Lewis: *Leonardo the Inventor*
Martin Lindsay: *The Epic of Captain Scott*
David Line: *Run for Your Life; Mike and Me; Under Plum Lake*
Kathleen Lines: *The House of the Nightmare; The Haunted and the Haunters*
Joan Lingard: *Across the Barricades; Into Exile; The Clearance; The File on Fräulein Berg*
Penelope Lively: *The Ghost of Thomas Kempe*
Jack London: *The Call of the Wild; White Fang*
Carson McCullers: *The Member of the Wedding*
Lee McGiffen: *On the Trail to Sacramento*
Margaret Mahy: *The Haunting*
Wolf Mankowitz: *A Kid for Two Farthings*
Jan Mark: *Thunder and Lightnings; Under the Autumn Garden*
James Vance Marshall: *A River Ran Out of Eden; Walkabout; My Boy John that Went to Sea; A Walk to the Hills of the Dreamtime*
David Martin: *The Cabby's Daughter*
John Masefield: *The Bird of Dawning; The Midnight Folk*
W. Somerset Maugham: *The Kite and Other Stories*
Guy de Maupassant: *Prisoners of War and Other Stories*
Laurence Meynell: *Builder and Dreamer*
Yvonne Mitchell: *Cathy Away*
Honoré Morrow: *The Splendid Journey*
R. K. Narayan: *A Tiger for Malgudi*
Bill Naughton: *The Goalkeeper's Revenge; A Dog Called Nelson; My Pal Spadger*
E. Nesbit: *The Railway Children; The Story of the Treasure Seekers*
E. Neville: *It's Like this, Cat*
Mary Norton: *The Borrowers*
Robert C. O'Brien: *Mrs Frisby and the Rats of NIMH; Z for Zachariah*
Scott O'Dell: *Island of the Blue Dolphins*
George Orwell: *Animal Farm*
Katherine Paterson: *Jacob Have I Loved; Bridge to Terabithia*